HOW I BECAME A SHAMMER:

The Part Of The Army That Was Not Shown In Commercials

Stay Strong and
follow your Dreams.
Be patient, Believe and
Say your Prayers.
Peace and Blessings.
one Love.

Leon H. Williams

Table Of Contents

Dedication

This book is dedicated to all of the soldiers, past, present and future, Army Strong. This book is also dedicated to the character who taught me everything I know, Ferris Bueller from Ferris Bueller's Day Off.

Shamology 101

Class Is In

Session

The Army is a great organization
It's just some of the people in it who
are able to make leadership decisions, are the
ones who makes it bad for everyone else
Sham Life

Chapter One

INTRODUCTION

Becoming a shammer[1] is not easy work, in fact it may take years
for someone to be able to learn everything that there is to know about
shamming. There is always that one soldier that seems to be nowhere
in sight when it's time to get shit done. You're probably wondering,
"How the hell does he get away with it?" I believe that in order to
master the skill of shamming, one must treat it as an art in order for
them to become a professional. The first step to becoming a shammer

---

[1] Shammer: a shammer is someone who is skilled at getting out of work. An individual who is a shammer is very clever and cunning. A shammer is someone who is able to invent new ways of how to get out of work. The shammer normally feels the reason for them leaving work is more important than them being there. A shammer is very good with communicating with people and through trial and error, has learned how to get his/her way. A shammer is a good observer of his environment and is able to quickly recognize and adapt to a changing system.

is by learning the system. Every duty station that you will go to will pretty much be the same. It is absolutely important that you make it on time to accountability formation because that is the time when the platoon sergeant and squad leaders will be looking for you. Sometimes your squad leader or platoon sergeant will cover down for you if you miss formation, but by them doing this may put their integrity on the line and could possibly get them into a lot of trouble if you are found somewhere that you should not be. One of the main reasons why having your immediate supervisors cover down for you is looked down upon is because of the possibility that you could be stuck somewhere in a ditch or worst, dead. Therefor if you intend on having your squad leader cover down for you, it would be best to give them a heads up by calling them a few minutes prior to the 0620 formation so that they will know that you are safe. It is important to note that just because you call your supervisor does not mean that you will not receive a negative counseling statement. In some circumstances the squad leader may give you a verbal counseling which could be an ass chewing, depending on how their feeling that day. One thing to keep in mind is that an ass chewing is much better than having your actions put on paper because your leadership can start a paper trail on you which can result in you getting chaptered out of the military. For some soldiers, they don't care if they receive a counseling statement because they want to get out of the Army but if I was put in this type of situation, I would choose the ass chewing over a counseling statement any day. One thing my old first sergeant used to tell me and some of the other soldiers was not to give someone the power to make a decision concerning your career. In other words, be smart and stay out of trouble. If your plan is to get out of the Army, try your hardest not to get out for disciplinary reasons. Instead, one of the best ways to get out is to fail a PT test or to bust tape. Reason being is because you can receive an honorable discharge for these two and still maintain all of your benefits. It's important to remember that you cannot receive an ETS award for being overweight but you can receive an award for failing the APFT. Command maintenance is normally done on Mondays after the 0930 work call formation. There are a number of reasons why soldiers hate performing command maintenance or preventive maintenance checks and services on vehicles. One of the reasons why is because most of the equipment in the motorpool[2] is

---

[2] Motor pool: The motor pool is where all of the military vehicles that belongs to a specific company or battalion are located. Included within the motor pool are the mechanics who not only works on the vehicles but also takes care of the generators as well.

dead-lined and has not moved since the soldier first arrived in the unit. Another reason why soldiers hate PMCS'ing their equipment every week is because they put the same faults on the 5988's and nothing ever gets changed. Because of this, soldiers may fill out a stack of 5988's which should take them hours to complete in a few minutes by putting the date on the 5988 which signifies that nothing is wrong with the equipment. Although this strategy works, it could cause a lot of suspicion if you turn in a bunch of 5988's with no faults on them and just have the date on it. For the remainder of the day, soldiers will hide out in the vehicle with the heater running, looking at Facebook on their phones until it's time for them to go to lunch. Depending on your military occupational specialty will determine how the rest of your day will go. For example, if you're a fueler or a water treatment specialist, you may be able to get away with a lot more than someone who works as a cook or a military police officer. Never the less, it is important to learn and recognize the system early so you can plan your strategy accordingly. If you know that your section does not have a lot of work to complete after lunch time, it might be a good idea to check with your squad leader to see if you can take care of personal business instead of sticking around at the job site. It is also important to note that you do not want to abuse this by asking to leave work every day because the other soldiers in your squad and/or platoon may notice that you are never at work and start complaining. Thus, instead of always asking if you can leave work, ask your squad leader if there's any work that needs to be done.

I know your probably saying to yourself, "why am I going to ask if there is any work to do if my main objective is to get out of work, but the thing that you need to understand is that by asking your squad leader if there is any work that needs to be done will cause them to think what needs to be done or you can ask them if they need any help with anything. This will show them that you care, whether you really do or don't. By showing your squad leader that you care and that you want to work may cause them to say "ok, help me with this or that". For this reason, when you ask them this question, you should go in hoping for the best but expecting the worse. In this case, the best case scenario would be for them to tell you that they don't need any help and to go home for the rest of the day. On the other hand, the worst case scenario would be that they are swamped with work, making it a long night for the two of you. You may have the type of sergeant who has a big ego and although they need help, will never accept you volunteering to help them.

Prior to asking your supervisor if they need any help or if there is anything that you can do, you should first make an analysis of the work area to ensure that nothing needs to get done. This way, this will increase your chances of being released. If you are going to sham, it's important that you stay active and use your time wisely. If your squad leader releases you and tells you to stay by your phone and that he or she will call you if they need you, take this time to do something productive. Occasionally, your squad leader may ask you where you are going, so you should have an answer ready when they ask you this. Some of the places that you can go without worrying so much about getting into trouble is going to the Ed Center, or the library. While you're there, you can work on correspondence courses or other military education. In addition to this, you can sign up for college courses. Some of the places that you should stay away from is the PX[3], bowling alley or any other place which is known as a social gathering

---

[3] PX, also known as the post exchange, are located on every military installation and is a place where soldiers, Department of Defense contractors and families can go to shop. The PX is very similar to Walmart except for the fact that everything is tax free.

area that high ranking officials may be at. One thing I have always said was if you were to ever get questioned about why you are somewhere else other than your place of duty, that you could easily reply by reversing the question and asking them why are they there instead of their place of duty. I must warn you that things can get pretty bad for you if you ask this question because it can make it seem as if you are being disrespectful and/or a smart ass. Thus try to avoid coming into contact with these types of individuals by not going to places like this. If you absolutely have to go to a place like this, such as Wal-Mart or Walgreens during duty hours, you should already have a plan put in place just in case you were to get questioned of why you are not at work.

Some of the things that you can say which can get you out of a jam are "hey sergeant, my wife asked me to pick her up some meds because she's feeling sick or I forgot to pack my child's lunch for school this morning, so I was just grabbing something really quick for them". Whatever lie you decide to come up with, make sure it's a good one. The last thing you would want to do is tell your sergeant or lieutenant (LT) that your wife is sick or kids need lunch for school and they know that you don't have kids and/or you have been divorced for over a year. Although it's really easy to lie and some people may be better at it than others, I believe that you should only do this on a case by case basis, otherwise, I strongly recommend that you tell the truth to people at all times because the truth is easier to remember. As long as your NCO's and or officers do not ever catch you in a lie, they will have no reason not to believe you. Thus, it is important to gain their trust and maintain it until you PCS[4].

---

[4] PCS- permanent change of station. This happens in a soldier career when they have fulfilled their obligation at a duty station and is ready to relocate. When a soldier PCS from duty station to duty station, their family will be able to go with them if they are married with children.

IS PT OVER YET

Sham Life

Chapter Two

Waking Up Late for PT

How many of us have found ourselves in this situation where we forget to set our alarm clock or we set our alarm but accidentally put it on P.M instead of A.M. Another thing is forgetting to charge our phones at night and so when we wake up late in the morning our phone is dead. Once we plug it in, we have several missed calls from different members of our leadership wondering where we are. One thing that always bugs me is when your squad leader cannot get a hold of you so they ask someone else to call you to see if you would answer for them, as if you have a problem with picking up the phone when your squad leader calls or something. In the case that you are questioned, you got to let them know the truth which is that you do not have a problem with answering the phone when they call, it was just that your phone was dead. It may be a good thing too for you to let them know that since you don't have an issue with answering their phone calls that they do not ask other people to call you. After telling this to your squad leader, they may respond with "you don't tell me what to do" or something along those lines to get you out of their face, but if they are cool and understanding, then they may accept your request.

Over the years I have often heard that the reason why a sergeant should not cover down for his soldiers when they are late is because they could be in a ditch, so my suggestion for this is that if you wake up one morning and see that you are late, go fall in a ditch. When doing so, make sure that you have your cellphone with you so you can call your squad leader and let him know. It's important to note: do not fall completely in the ditch. What you would do is:

1. Open up the ditch and put your leg in it.

2. Make sure that the ditch is somewhere close to where your formation is going to be held at, that way you can say that it happened while you were in route to formation

3. Call your squad leader and pretend that you're in pain and you're not sure if you can move. I want you to note that 1 of 2 things will happen at that time. He or she may tell you to keep them updated on your injury or 2, they will come check on you to see if they can help. Now having them come see you may not be a good idea, so if they suggest if you want him to go check on you, tell him to hold on a minute so you can see if you can move

The purpose of doing this is to buy you some extra time to get to formation, so try not to spend too much time talking. I want you to keep in mind that this idea may be good to use only one time or else they may begin to get suspicious. Another thing that happens all too often which makes soldiers be late for PT[5] or morning formation is that they forget to set the volume on their phone because the day prior

---

[5] PT- In the Army soldiers are required to be physically fit to ensure that they are capable of meeting the demands of war. Soldiers are required to conduct mandatory PT Monday through Friday in a squad, platoon or company element. Soldiers who demonstrate excellence in PT may be allowed to conduct PT on their own as an incentive for their hard work. Each PT session may last for roughly 90 minutes.

they put their phone volume on vibrate or silent while they were standing in formation and forget to turn the volume back up, once formation is complete. I remember a few years ago when I was stationed at Fort Campbell in Kentucky, the power used to always go out on base, at least once a month. Sometimes the power would go out in the middle of the night which shut the power off on my alarm clock, causing me to over sleep.

There are a number of things which can happen to you which causes you to oversleep and it is very possible that they can all happen on the same day. Because of this, here are a few things that you can do to help prevent you from missing formation. The first thing you may want to consider is buying yourself two alarm clocks. The reason why you want to buy two alarm clocks is because you may hit the snooze button on one of them every 5 or 10 minutes before the First Sergeant (1SG)[6] has his formation and by the time you realize what time it is, you are already late or about to be late. If you have 2 alarm clocks, be sure to place them in different areas within your room, that way it will

---

[6] First Sergeant- also abbreviated as 1SG, is the senior ranking Sergeant within your company. Due to the way that promotions are set up in the Army, the 1SG is the senior ranking enlisted member in the company because of his rank and not because of the amount of time that he has been in the military.

take you some time and effort to turn them off. For example, you may want to put one of them on your bathroom sink and the other one on your dresser. It is important to put an alarm clock somewhere where it will cause you to get up out of your bed and shut it off compared to keeping it in arms reach where you can easily hit the snooze button and fall back to sleep. I personally used three alarm clocks at once, one of which was my cell phone and the other two were the portable kind that you plug into the wall. This is a workable solution that you can use to prevent you from being FTR (failure to report).

Although I can think of other things in life that are worse than being FTR, such as getting shot, waking up in the morning opening your eyes and the first thing that you notice is that it's 0640 and your already 10 minutes late to PT formation can be one of the worst feelings that a good soldier can have because ultimately it's their fault and preventable. If you are anything like me, then the first thing that comes to your mind when you first wake up and notice that you're late is "OH SHIT". Depending on how late you are, you may begin wondering what is your company or platoon doing at that moment. Mondays, Wednesdays and Fridays are normally run days and Tuesday/Thursday are muscular strength and endurance (muscle failure) days. If it's past the 0630 formation time, you will realize that

there is no use of trying to contact anybody because no one will have

their cell phones on them during PT. You can call your squad leader

and leave a message which details that you lost your keys and had your

cell phone in the car and as long as you don't have a history of being

FTR, it is possible that this may work. If you decide not to take

the time to call you're squad leader so that you can hurry up and get

there, then you must be ready to explain yourself once you see him in

person because you know that an ass chewing[7] is coming.

Depending on the duty station that you're currently at, one option

that you can take is to rush to sick call and tell them that you're feeling

sick. When your squad leader ask where have you been, you can tell them

that you went to sick call and that you thought you told them the day

prior. This technique could be known as the okeydokey or pulling a fast

one on your leadership. Although this might work and get you out of

receiving a negative counseling statement, your squad leader or leadership

---

[7] Ass Chewing: an ass chewing is when your supervisor or someone else of authority finds a fault that you committed and verbally criticizes you. The purpose of an ass chewing is to let you know what you did wrong and give you an opportunity to fix yourself.

may say that you should have known better than but they most likely will

let it slide. If it turns out that you do not have a sick call at your duty

station, you can go to the ER. If you tell them that you are throwing up or

that you have diarrhea, they may give you an electrolyte solution and

quarters[8]. I know that lying is wrong and if you're afraid of how it might

affect your conscience, then don't do it. Just be aware that you may get

hemmed up for being late and given some sort of corrective training and

some NCO'S can be very creative at giving corrective training, so you

decide.

---

[8] Quarters: Soldiers are given quarters when they are sick or injured as a way of providing them with time to heal. Normally a doctor or physician assistant will give a soldier quarters for 24-72 hours depending on the circumstance. When soldiers are on quarters, they are not required to return to work until their quarters has expired.

Chapter Three

Sick Call Ranger

A sick call ranger is someone who is always getting injured or sick and gets out of physical training to go to sick call. There is a stigma which is placed on soldiers who go to sick call because some see it as a sign of weakness. This attitude makes many soldiers refrain from going to sick call because of what others may think of them. One thing to remember and that I always say is that "if you're sick, you're sick" what this means is that if you're really sick, you should get checked out by the doctor to make sure that your good because if you don't get checked out by a medical professional and keep pushing yourself, then 2 things are going to happen: 1) your leadership is going to make you do PT anyway despite your injury because you don't have a profile stating that you cannot do certain exercises or 2) you're going to make your injury worse which could put you out of the fight even longer once you seek medical attention. But you will see which soldiers are always on quarters and which ones suck it up. You will also recognize which physician assistants (PA) will just give you Motrin and which ones will actually give you time to heal. One thing that I

recognized is that if you ask your PA for 24 hour quarters, they may

give it to you, so don't be afraid to ask. If you go to sick call for a

legitimate reason but one that is not life threatening to the point where

you can barely move, its ok for you to sit back and relax until your

name is called.

Depending on where your stationed at, it is also possible that

there will be so many soldiers at sick call, that you wouldn't get seen

until a few minutes before its time for you to go to lunch. This is

different from malingering where you pretend to be sick but you're

really fine. It's important to note that malingering is punishable under

the uniform code of military justice if you are found guilty of this

offense. Keep in mind that the scenario I described above is not

malingering but rather taking your sweet time to get seen by a provider

by putting your name at the bottom of the list and letting everyone

else get seen before you, making you the last soldier or the second to

last soldier to be seen by the provider before lunch time. The good

thing about this type of situation is that when your squad leader calls

you, you can tell them the truth, which is that you're still at sick call

waiting to be seen. That way if they decide to come up there to check on you to make sure that you're indeed telling the truth, they can see

that you are and will leave you alone so you can continue chilling.

Chapter Four

Making Appointments

Making appointments can be a great way of getting out of work. It is not uncommon for a soldier to have 2 appointments on the same day or have an appointment that last all day. I know you may be wondering "how can an appointment last all day" and the technique to doing this really falls in the strategy that you use. For example, if you schedule an appointment that is an hour away from base, what you would do is schedule it for after PT, say around 11am. I think that 11am is a good time to schedule an appointment because by it being an hour away means that you will not be required to show up to work call at 0930. So after driving for an hour to make it to your appointment on time, let's say that your appointment last for an hour.

Now it is 12:00, well you know that your company goes to lunch from 1200 – 1330, so you go ahead and take your 90 minute lunch break before hitting the road. Now it's 1330 and you're ready for your drive back to post. Let's say on your way back you hit minimal traffic and make it back to base around 1500, to arrive at your unit at 1515. This will leave you with an hour and 15 minutes to an hour and 45 minutes before everyone is released. When you make it back to the unit, it's important that you thank your squad leader for letting you take care of your business. After doing so, you should go see what work needs to be done. Hopefully when you get back, it's a pretty slow day and your squad leader tells you it's a platoon release, meaning everyone will be leaving early. In that case, you pretty much had an easy day. This is just one example of how appointments can work in your favor for getting out of work.

It is important to note that although making appointments are great, they can also get you in trouble. I know you might be asking yourself "how in the hell can making appointments get me in trouble" and the answer to this is, by making so many appointments that you mess around and do not show up for one of them. If you miss an appointment in the Army, you already know that everybody and their momma is going to be in your business, asking why you missed an appointment and the unit may have you do all types of crazy shit like stand in front of the PX with your dress blues on and greet everyone as they walk into the building or your unit leadership may have a fuck it type of attitude and recommend you for an Article 15[9].

I first did not understand why leaders cared so much about soldiers missing appointments but then I found out the answer and it all made sense. One reason why your leadership care so much is because missing an appointment cost the army millions of dollars a year. Think about it this way, when you miss an appointment that was already scheduled for you, that 30 minutes or hour block is still going to result in the provider getting paid. For example, if 8 soldiers schedule an appointment with Dr. X from 0800-1700 and it completely fills up his schedule for the day but they all cancel and/or a no show, then he just got paid a full day salary for doing absolutely nothing but showing up. By multiplying this by all of the missed appointments that occur each day, will result in millions of dollars wasted.

---

[9] Article 15: There are 3 types of Article 15's which are company; summarized and field grade. An Article 15 is Non-judicial punishment that commanders are authorized to use to discipline their soldiers. Soldiers who receive an Article 15 may receive 50% pay for 45 days, 45 days of extra duty from the hours of 1800-2300, reduction in rank and restriction from leaving the military installation for up to 45 days. A field grade Article 15 will stay on the soldier record while they are in the military, whereas a company grade Article 15 will come off the soldier record once they PCS to a new duty station.

If you are going to make a lot of appointments, be sure to put some type of system in place such as writing them down on the board in your platoon office or giving a copy of your appointment slip to your squad leader. Although these are great ways to ensure that you don't miss your appointments, you may want to take it a step further by creating your own appointment tracker. You can easily do this by purchasing a white board from the PX or Walmart and writing them down or putting sticky notes on the board as a reminder of all your appointments. It's important to note that you cannot solely rely on the automated appointment line to give you a reminder phone call because sometimes they will and sometimes they won't. So make sure that you take charge and be proactive when it comes to making appointments so that you do not become another victim.

Another great way to get out of work is if you have children. I know some of yall might think that using children to get out of work is messed up but it's an option. The military tries to give you every opportunity possible to take care of your family needs. Because of this, the more activities that your child is involved in the better. Examples of this will include parent teacher conferences, having to drop your children off at day care or pick them up early or anytime that your children get sick and you have to pick them up from school. All of these are great examples of how you can get out of work. One thing in particular that the Army allow, is for female soldiers to take 12 weeks of paid leave off from work after giving birth. Male soldiers on the other hand will only receive 10 days of paid leave after their wife has given birth, but hey time off is time off and you're getting paid so you really can't beat that. I have had soldiers who got pregnant on purpose the moment they found out the unit was deploying, for a chance that they wouldn't have to deploy to a combat area. If they time it right, they could potentially miss the entire deployment.

We have all heard of toxic leadership and can probably spot a dozen Non-Commissioned Officers who are real butt holes on and off of duty. It is possible that they can cause you to be so stressed out that you enroll yourself in behavior health. Sitting down and talking with a professional counselor can be very good for you to express your feelings and overcome any oppression that you may be experiencing. I believe that toxic leadership can cause a soldier to feel so oppressed that they begin to feel suppressed which ultimately makes them depressed. Going to behavior health will allow you to schedule such appointments as stress management and anger management, which may fall on separate days throughout the week. Not only will this serve as a benefit for your mental health but will also get you out of work for a few hours. Some soldiers already know this and will take full advantage of this opportunity, whereas others will schedule multiple behavior health appointments because they genuinely have behavior issues that they cannot control on their own.

Regardless of the reason why you schedule behavior health appointments, it is important to note that many times soldiers are labeled by their peers as being crazy. They may make fun of your disorder and may even alienate you, making you feel as if you are an outcast and not part of the team. One thing that can cause your peers to make fun of you is if you are taking psychiatric medications to help reduce your anxiety. Thus, if you find yourself in this type of situation, the best thing to do may be to keep people out of your personal business. One thing to keep in mind about the military is that "there are no secrets in the Army". What this means is that everybody knows everyone else's business. Because of this, it is important to only tell those who you can trust about your personal business. One thing that I always say is "people will only know what you tell them" so unless you just have a big mouth and have to tell people everything that has ever happened to you, keep some things to yourself. Before telling

someone something, take a moment and think "what good is it going

to do me by telling this person some particular thing. My grandmother

always told me to think 5 times before you speak, that way you don't

say something you end up regretting later.

<u>Chapter Five</u>

<u>Know Who Your Friends Are</u>

One thing that I was told when I was a private was that the NCO's are not your friend. Now you may find some that are cool, who you can joke around with and you will find some who will say a joke about you but get offended when you say a joke about them. Now don't get me wrong, I have a lot of respect for the role of the NCO because they have so many expectations that they have to deal with on a day to day basis. Take your NCO for example, he or she may have 5 or 10 soldiers under their charge that they are responsible for. If a soldier doesn't get a haircut, they have to answer for it; if the soldier didn't shave prior to showing up for PT formation, they have to answer for it and if their soldier doesn't make it on time for their appointment, you guessed it, they have to answer for it.

Now when your squad leader is being questioned by the platoon sergeant or first sergeant about why you are looking ate the hell up[10], he or she may think to themselves "I don't know why in the hell he didn't shave this morning and I really don't give a shit" but the typical response he gives Top (Trainer of professionals) is that he will fix it. Aside from answering for you for all the times you fuck up, they also have to be a role model to guide you on the right path, a counselor when your girlfriend breaks up with you, a financial accountant when you don't pay your bills on time and a fitness instructor to make sure that you are not a fat body. The list can go on and on but the main thing to remember is your squad leader doesn't get paid to like you; their primary job is to train and lead you. It is also important to remember that they were once privates themselves and can probably read through the bullshit that you are getting ready to tell them because chances are they have either heard it before or they have used the excuses themselves.

You might get some sergeants who pretend that they were never ate up before or may claim that they have not been late to formation. Do me a favor and don't believe that shit. The reason why

---

[10] Ate up: a term most commonly used by sergeants to describe a soldier whose appearance is not in accordance with Army regulation 670-1. If a soldier uniform and boots are dirty, their name tape is falling off of their jacket and patrol cap because the Velcro is worn out and their cargo pockets are unfastened, the sergeant may some something like "hey private, your uniform is ate the fuck up, go fix yourself".

they lie to you by telling you this is because they are supposed to be the example. For this reason it is important for you to have a good lie when you are trying to get out of work. Simply telling your sergeant "a ser'ent[11], I don't feel like coming in to work today", might not be the best thing to say to them unless you want to get cussed out. The truth to the matter is, 9 times out of 10, your sergeant probably doesn't want to be at work either but for whatever reason, they continue to **EMBRACE THE SUCK** and show up to work anyway. Never the less, know who your talking to before you talk to them. If your sergeant is near retirement or getting ready to PCS, they may be easier to talk to and you may be able to get your way more often, as compared to a brand new sergeant who recently got promoted and has something to prove.

One thing to keep in mind is that sergeants are not the only ones who are not paid to be your friend. This also applies to your peers who stand on the left and right of you. Although your battle buddies are supposed to have your back in good times and in war, you always have those ones who are blue falcons (Buddy Fuckers). You cannot trust a blue falcon, because they will snitch on you faster than a

---

[11] Sar'ent: slang for sergeant.

speeding bullet. But don't think that it's just the blue falcons and the sergeants that you have to worry about. Majority of people who you come across will believe that it is either you or them. They may not necessarily have a problem with you shamming out on work but when they are confronted about your whereabouts, they may give you up to protect themselves.

One of the reasons why they snitch on you is not because they don't like you or something like that but simply because if your squad leader finds out where you really are and determines that your buddy is lying for you, then both of yall can be in deep shit. Can you blame them, well I will leave that up to you to decide, but keep this in mind when making your decsion, do you honestly want your buddy to go down for some stupid shit that you got yourself into? If you answered yes to this question, then you may want to look in the mirror because you could be the blue falcon and not even know it.

It may turn out that you only have 2 or 3 people who you share mutual trust with. These friends could be considered your ride or die type of people who you would do anything for without hesitation. My advice is to try to encourage each other to do more positive things in their lives than negative things but always have your brother's or sister's back, NO MATTER WHAT. If you are going to

sham together, then you all need to be on the same sheet of music and

have your stories straight, just in case you get caught. The worse thing

that yall can do if both of yall are caught up, is one person say you all

went to the gym and the other person tell the truth, that yall went back

to the barracks because it wasn't nothing to do at work. So make sure

your story is good and everyone is tracking what to say before yall start

making any moves.

Chapter Six

Out Of Sight, Out Of

Mind

When your squad leader tells you to be "out of sight out of mind" that does not mean for you to be at the PX shopping or at GameStop looking at the new video games that just came out. No, that means for you to take your butt to your room and stay there until either 1) They call you and say to come back to work or 2) it's the end of the day and time for everyone to go home. It might be a good idea to give your squad leader a phone call before changing out of your ACU's and getting into civilian clothes, just to make sure that everyone is officially released for the day. That could be a quick way for one person to mess it up for everyone else, if you are caught in civilian clothes shopping on or off post while the rest of the unit is still working.

Like I said in a previous chapter, 9 times out of 10, your squad leader may not want to be at work themselves but when one of his soldiers gets caught doing the wrong thing when he tried to unofficially give them time off to go to their rooms and chill until further notice, then expect to hear your squad leader say something along the lines of "I tried to give yall time off, but yall messed it up, so now we have a lot of eyes on us". Meaning I cannot give yall no more free time for a while until we can show that we can do the right thing again. So to prevent you and your squad from getting into trouble and taking any unnecessary hits, a few things that you should do is:

1. Keep your phone on you at all times and make sure it's charged.

2. Stay in uniform until told otherwise.

3. Stay within a 10 to 15 minute radius of the company or motor pool.

4. Don't fall asleep before setting an alarm to wake you up 30 minutes prior to C.O.B

5. Don't get drunk or consume any alcohol once so ever.

6. Don't go telling people that you are off, especially in a bragging manner.

7. Don't stay at work or around your work area while the rest of your squad has already left.

8. Don't do nothing stupid that's going to get you in trouble with the military police or civilian police.

9. Don't be in a high visibility area where high ranking officials may be and/or their spouses because they can identify you by the unit patch you wear.

10. Stay out of sight, out of mind.

By following these ten steps you will be doing your part to ensure that you and your squad is good.

If you are stopped by someone higher ranking than you and they ask you what are you doing at a particular place, you got to be quick on your feet with a response that is believable. An example of this could be to tell whoever it is that's questioning you that your squad leader told everyone to come back to the barracks to prepare their equipment for a TA50[12] layout. Whatever reason you give the individual, make sure that everyone else is tracking so you all don't

---

[12] TA50: TA50 is a table of allowances that each soldier is given which has all of the individual equipment that they are issued upon arrival into the Army. As a soldier goes from duty station to duty station, they will either be required to turn in equipment or be issued new equipment. The individual equipment issued to soldiers includes things such as Kevlar (helmet), IBA (bullet proof vest), EYEPRO (ballistic glasses), Sleeping Bag, etc.

get caught up. Again this falls in line with ensuring that everyone is on the same page before yall take off. My old commander used to always tell the company during a safety brief[13] the importance of the 7 P's. The 7 P's are (proper prior planning prevents piss poor performance). It is also important to remember that men never plans on failing, but it is not uncommon to see a man who failed to plan. Thus, as long as you and your guys have a solid plan, this should ensure a successful execution.

---

[13] Safety Brief: a safety brief is conducted in the Army on the last day of each week prior to the soldiers being released for the weekend. Safety briefs held at the company level will either be conducted by the company commander or 1SG, but can be given by the soldiers that are standing within their formation. Safety briefs are given to let soldiers know what not to do over the weekend that could cause them to get in trouble. Common topics of discussion includes: use protection, If it doesn't belong to you, don't touch it, don't beat your family or pets, don't drink and drive or leave your drinks unattended at a club.

Chapter Seven

Let Us Go

How many times have you come in for 0930 work call but there was no work for you to do. You have already PMCS'ed the vehicles for command maintenance and done everything else that your leadership told you to do and so now you and the platoon are just sitting inside of the motor pool or office area doing nothing but looking at Facebook until it's time to go to lunch. You go to lunch and come back to work on time and sit back in the same seat that you were in before you left. An hour or 2 past by and now it's getting time for everyone to go home but right before it's time for yall to leave, your squad leader or platoon sergeant comes in and says "hey yall, we got a mission that needs to get done before anyone can leave for the day". You think to yourself or may say under your breath that this is some straight up bull shit. How come they couldn't tell us this shit 2 hours ago when we wasn't doing nothing but just sitting here. A soldier may go on to say "see this the type of shit that I be talking about, that's why I'm happy I'm getting out, so I don't have to deal with this shit no more".

Some people may say "what are you complaining about, you haven't done nothing all day" and even though that statement is true, that we have not done any work all day, that is beside the point. Working doesn't really bother me, what bothers me is why they have to wait until the last minute to tell us to do something. I found out a long time ago that soldiers will complain if they have too much work to do and they will complain if they don't have any work to do at all. A few years ago I brought this problem up to my dad and he said "well son, your' getting paid to do nothing, do you know how many people would love to work for a place that paid them to sit around all day". I agreed with him because I knew he was telling the truth, that most of the time we are getting paid to do nothing but sit around and talk to each other, but then you may think to yourself "what am I doing with my life". I'm wasting my time here doing nothing.

So in reference to the above scenario, the soldier may realize that there is really nothing that they can do about it at that moment besides getting up and doing whatever task it was that their squad leader told them to do and do it quickly so that they can go home. So let's say that 2 weeks may pass by and the same thing happens again where you get told at the last minute that there is a job that needs to get done and then again you get told at the last minute that a job needs to get done 2 weeks after that and the cycle continues to go on and on. If this happens, the soldier may say to himself "what the hell is going on, this place is so unorganized". Some soldiers may be brave enough to voice their opinions to their squad leader or platoon sergeant for which one of two things will normally happen. The first thing that might happen is that your squad leader will blame it on the platoon sergeant or the platoon sergeant will blame it on the first sergeant and commander by saying something along the lines of "I get the information and pass it down to yall. The second thing that may happen when you voice your opinions is that they tell you to shut the hell up and do what they tell you to do, unless you want a counseling statement for not participating.

Regardless of how your supervisors respond to you, you may say to yourself that you are going to report it on the command climate survey[14]. You could also voice your opinions during your next census

---

[14] Command Climate Survey: unit commanders are authorized to use this tool as a way of measuring their unit's morale and how well things are going within the unit. The command climate survey consist of 95 questions that each soldier assigned to a unit must

session, but generally everyone is quiet at those until one or two soldiers begin talking before everyone else starts to voice their concerns regarding the company. You will be amazed by how many people share the same gripes and complaints as you. After everyone has voiced their concerns and the first sergeant has jotted down his notes, he will tell everyone something along the lines of "I got it" or "ill fix it" and then he will go and speak with the NCO's to hear their complaints and then the 1SG and the company commander will come up with a plan on how to fix it. Things may or may not get better depending on what it is. For example, if the problem is something regarding sharp issues or EO, then rest assured that there is a 0 tolerance for that type of behavior within a unit, even if the 1SG or commander are the ones that are being accused of doing such crimes. If you ever find yourself in this type of situation and feel that your EO rights have been violated, I recommend you see the battalion EO[15] representative immediately.

---

complete. It is important for soldiers to answer the questions truthfully so that the unit commanders will know which areas needs the most attention.

[15] Equal Opportunity: also known as EO, ensures that all members of the military to include spouses and DA (Department of the Army) civilians will be treated with respect, regardless of race, religion, gender and sexual beliefs. The equal opportunity policy is to be followed 24 hours a day, on and off the military installation.

Let's say though that one of the issues brought to the table was the fact that there was not enough work to do to last for an entire day, Monday through Friday and that doing busy work such as sweeping up rocks within the motor pool or cleaning the windows on vehicles that are dead-lined[16] and/or don't get driven because you don't have enough licensed drivers in your platoon, is a waste of not only the soldiers energy but their time as well; when they can be doing something better. So the 1SG may tell the platoon sergeant "ok, if there's nothing going on past 15:00, go ahead and release your soldiers. That's good news. Now everyone is happy until the 1SG and/or platoon sergeant PCS and things go back to how they were before. So the question is, why won't they just let us go home and call us if they need us and how come they won't plan what the tasking's are a week prior so that we (soldiers) are always actively engaged in work. Well you know what they say in the army "if it makes too much sense, then something must be wrong".

---

[16] Deadlined: A piece of military equipment that is inoperative due to electrical malfunctions or major damage which needs to be repaired. A military vehicle may be deadlined due to a safety reason such as the horn not working or because it doesn't have any running lights. In this type of situation, it is the decision of the commander to allow that piece of equipment to travel on the road.

Many years ago, I found out that of the 6 or 7 hours that we are at work, we may only have about 2 hours of actual work to do, if everyone is actively engaged. But what tends to happen is the two hours of work that we actually have is spread out and made to last for 6 or 7 hours. You may be saying "well how is this even possible and why. Well, one reason this happens is because the last thing that your first sergeant will want to see is a bunch of his soldiers doing a whole lot of nothing, so he calls in the platoon sergeant and tells him to fix the problem. The platoon sergeant will then let his squad leaders know what is going on and after going back and forth about how there is just not enough work to do for the soldiers on a daily basis, the squad leader will say roger[17] and will creatively make a plan.

It is possible that you may be in a MOS[18] that is not needed within your company and so you may feel like you are not really learning anything or doing what you signed up for. Because of this, if you wanted to get out of the Army and get a civilian job that is similar

---

[17] Roger: There may be several different meanings for the term ROGER, but the one that I find which makes the most sense is Received Order Given, Expect Results.
[18] MOS: An MOS or Military Occupational Specialty, is the job that a soldier enlist for when they join the Army. In the Army there are over 210 jobs that a soldier can choose from. An MOS that is combat oriented such as Infantry will generally have lower promotion standards than other MOS's, which means that a soldier will get promoted faster if they are in a combat MOS.

to what you did in the military, you wouldn't know what to do. If you find yourself in this type of situation, you will have an important decision to make which is "should I change my MOS and try to get a job that I will actually do or should I continue working in this MOS and reenlist, to only continue doing nothing but collecting a pay check every two weeks. The other option that you may decide is to take your chances and get out. I believe that many people will decide to stay in the Army because they are afraid of getting out. Most soldiers don't have a college degree or take advantage of the free college tuition assistance program because they feel they don't have the time right now to go to school, which to me is a bunch of bullshit but ill get into that later. Without a college education and with the way the economy is right now, may persuade many soldiers to decide to stay in the military as long as possible because in their eyes, no one is going to hire them with a starting salary of what their currently making.

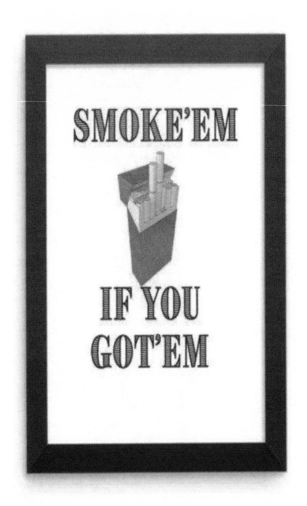

Chapter Eight

Smoke Break

Smoke'em if you got'em. One way that NCO's help pass the time is by giving the soldiers breaks throughout the work day. For example, on any given day, you show up 10 minutes prior to the 0930 work call and see your squad leader. After he does his checks to make sure everyone is there and in the right uniform he says "ok guys, go ahead and hang tight for a few minutes while I get some paper work together. One of the soldiers ask, "A ser'ent, is it cool if we smoke and 9 times out of 10 the answer will probably be yes. 10-15 minutes pass, it's now 10 o'clock and the sergeant is ready for you to come back and get started working. The work that the sergeant gives you last for an hour and now you have 30 minutes left before its time to go to lunch. After the sergeant inspects the job you just done to make sure everything is good, he tells you to take another break. So out of the 2 ½ hours that you were at work, you actually only worked for 1 hour or 40%. The other 60% of your time was either spent talking, smoking and/or Facebooking.

After returning from your 90 minute lunch break, your squad leader say's ok we got a mission. We need to spray paint all the bumper numbers in the motor pool. So after spending 30 minutes to find some spray paint, if you are lucky, you then got to find stencils. It always seem to amaze me that every time we have to spray paint bumper numbers, we are given a drip pan full of stencils with all different sizes of numbers and letters. After looking through 100's of stencils, you would be lucky to find all the letters and numbers you need to make a complete set. If not, then you will have to make your own out of a manila folder; sometimes substituting backwards S for the number 2 and a lowercase L for the number 1. So after spending an hour or so to gather all of the equipment needed to successfully spray paint the bumper numbers. It is now time to execute.

Due to the fact that you are limited supplies and only need about 4 soldiers to accomplish this task but since you have a platoon of 40-50 people, everyone comes outside to watch. Before you guys get started, the squad leader ask "ok who wants to volunteer to do the spray painting", someone in the group may make a racist comment by saying "give it to the Mexican, because you know he used to tag on walls before he joined the military" or the African American soldier may volunteer to spray paint but does a bad job and someone

comments "man, I thought you would be a pro at this". Everybody

may laugh and joke except for the soldier or group who the joke is

referring to. It's ok to laugh and joke but just be careful to not offend

anyone because you can have an EO complaint against you real quick

if someone hears something they don't like.

So you start spray painting the bumper numbers and you get

about 4 or 5 done out of 30 vehicles. So after two hours of working,

it's now time to go home and the squad leader says that yall will finish

up tomorrow or we can stay late and try to get it all finished with the

promise of a comp day. You and your team already know that taking

the promise of a comp day is a 50/50 chance. The other issue you may

run into by working late is that if you're a meal card holder[19], then you

risk the chance of not making it to the DFAC[20] on time. So you ask

your squad leader "hey sarge, are we gonna have time to make it to the

DFAC" and he responds with these 3 letters that gives everyone

---

[19] Meal Card Holder: Single soldiers who are not married will be issued a meal card for them to eat in the DFAC. If they choose not to eat in the DFAC, they are still charged the full rate which increases every year. Married soldiers are given the food money in their paychecks which is a little above $350 per month.

[20] DFAC: also known as the dining facility. The army DFAC is very similar to a cafeteria. Each military base that a soldier is stationed at will have a DFAC for the soldiers to go eat at.

diarrhea, MRE. So yall work until its dark outside and cant spray paint anymore and then you ask your squad leader, "so are we good for our comp time tomorrow" and he says yes, take PT off and I'll see you at 0930. Although you were expecting to have the next day off, you settle for taking PT off so you can sleep in an extra hour or 2, plus it's a run day and your still feeling sore from the last 4 miles that yall ran the day prior.

Although you had a pretty easy day, you still feel like there is no reason why yall should have been working so late and that your NCO's should have had all this shit ready to go before he gave yall orders[21] so that you could have gotten the job done before COB[21]. You may think to yourself "what the hell is going on here", is it possible that my NCO's are shaming and that's the reason why shit can't get done on time and the answer is hell yeah. Sergeants are some of the biggest shammers that you will ever meet and the thing is, they can probably get away with it a lot easier than you because they don't have as many people to answer to like you do. But remember, NCO's were once privates too and probably felt and did the same things like you are doing now. I know your probably saying "well if that's the case, why don't they get their shit together instead of continuously making life worse for us and if you ask him what the hell is going on in a respectable and tactfully manner, they will probably tell you something along the lines of "man you know shit runs downhill, and when I get the information I push it down to yall". In addition to this, he may sympathize with you and tell you that he can't stand this shit either, but doing so may cause you to look at not only your squad leader differently but all NCO's in your chain of command differently, so I caution the NCO from doing this. Unless you guys have that type of

---

[21] COB: stands for Close of business. This is normally around 1630-1700 and is the time when everyone is supposed to get off of work every day.

relationship. Again, it's important to know the person you're talking to.

Chapter Nine

<u>Going To The Soldier Of The</u>

<u>Month Board</u>

I highly encourage all soldiers to take advantage of all the opportunities that being selected as the soldier of the month has to offer. One great benefit that you can receive by being selected as the soldier of the month is that it can get you out of work. Would you like to know how, well guess what, you're in luck. You already know that every month, theirs a soldier of the month board. Normally, when the squad leaders ask will anyone like to volunteer to go to the board, no one raises their hand. If this happens then one of two things may happen. You may get voluntold to go because each platoon is required to send at least 1 representative or the platoon sergeant may ask the squad leaders who they think is deserving enough to go to the board. In this case, unless your high speed or your squad leader likes you, you probably won't get chosen, so your best option is to raise your hand when the squad leader ask for volunteers. I mean, you should want to volunteer anyway because of all the good shit that I am about to tell you but before I go into all the benefits you will receive, I should first warn you that it involves a lot of studying.

I remember back in the day when I was competing for the soldier of the month board, I studied all day, hell, I even studied when I went on leave in California. I studied so much to the point where I felt I was like a walking study guide. Thanks to all the countless hours of studying, I was company soldier of the month, battalion soldier of the quarter, and brigade soldier of the quarter. I missed the soldier of the year board by one point because I took my class B dress shirt to the cleaners and forgot to put my name tag back on. Once I lost, I started to focus more on college. Now that I got that out of the way let's start talking about these rewards and how going to the board can get you out of work.

Due to the fact that most soldiers don't want to go to the soldier of the month board for whatever reason, by you raising your hand and volunteering already sets you apart from the rest of your peers and your leadership knows this. Regardless of how big your platoon is, you are the only one that is doing more than the rest of your battle buddies who are just doing PT, coming to work and going home every day, and guess what, when you come close to hitting your 18 month mark, I can almost guarantee that your name will be put in the running to receive a waiver for specialist. Things like going to the board, keeping your room clean, scoring high on your PT test[22] and not having any article 15's, will all increase your chances of receiving a waiver.

One thing I recommend when going to the board is first stopping by the Shoppette[23] and buying you about 2 or 3 packs of the 100 count note cards and a pack of ink pens with various colors. I find that reading board questions written in black ink seems dull and causes you to get tired quickly, as compared to reading in blue or red ink. One thing that you may want to try is writing the question in black ink and writing the answer in blue ink .Switch it up a little bit so you can stay focused. A few common ways that you can acquire a study guide

---

[22] PT test: also known as the Army physical fitness test (APFT), is a test given to soldiers every 6 months to ensure that the soldiers can pass the 2 mile run, push up event and sit up event. Soldiers who fail one of these events will be given time to pass the event in remedial PT before they are discharged from the Army. The grading for the APFT are separated in groups by the soldier's age. Soldiers must maintain a passing grade of 60% in each event in order to receive a GO.

[23] Shoppette: depending on the location, the shoppette is a convenience store which may also include a gas station located outside. The shoppette does not charge their shoppers taxes on the merchandise sold in the store.

is by first asking your squad leader if he has one. The second way is by

going to the clothing and sales store and purchasing one for about

$10. One thing to keep in mind though is, if you buy your study guide

from clothing and sales, just know that what you're buying is not a

complete study guide; Although it is a valuable resource to have and

keep within your home library. Another way of acquiring a study guide

is by going online to www.armystudyguide.com and printing it off

from there.

One thing I always did when I printed the study guide off of

the website was purchase a 3 ring binder and clear document

protectors. It is important to note that the complete study guide has

over 2,000 questions in it and is a little over three hundred pages, so

one thing I used to do to prevent using a lot of paper and ink was to

click the print tab on your computer and change the page layout to 4

pages on 1. Now that you have your study guide printed out, it's now

time to start making your note cards. One thing to remember about

the board is that the questions generally stay the same month after

month and one way to verify this is by looking at the LOI[24] for the

---

[24] LOI: this stands for Letter of Instruction or Letter of Intent. It is a packet that is given to the soldiers who will be attending the board. It includes the time, date and location where

previous months to see what questions the company 1SG or battalion command sergeants major asked. Due to the fact that the questions being asked generally remain the same month after month, you may want to hook up with someone who just went to the board or get with your squad leader to find out which questions are normally being asked at the board out of the 2,000 questions that are within the study guide.

I found out that of the 2,000 questions that are in the study guide, about 200 of those questions are generally chosen by the board members and each board member may only ask you 10-15 questions. So it would behoove you to seek out this information so that you only study the questions that they may ask you instead of trying to study everything. Don't get me wrong, the information contained within the study guide is some good knowledge that every soldier should know, but because your board date may be right around the corner, you really don't have time to waste. After making your note cards, bring them with you everywhere and keep them in your cargo pocket. The goal that you should be trying to achieve is to have everyone see you study,

---

the board will be convened and includes the sections which will be covered by the board members.

every day, that way nobody can say anything when they are stuck

working and you are off chilling because you got permission to study.

If it's too loud at your job where you are studying at, you can ask your

squad leader if you can go study somewhere else because you cannot

focus where you are. Most of the time, he/she will let you go as long

as there's not a lot of work that needs to get done which requires

everyone's help. Now if your squad leader gives you time off to study,

don't feel bad that you have been given the opportunity to be in a nice

and quiet place to study while everyone else is stuck working because

for 1) they all had the same opportunity as you to raise their hand and

volunteer to go to the board but they choose not to and for 2) you

have to remember that you are not only representing your squad but

your representing your platoon as well, when your competing at the

company level.

Once you win the company soldier of the month board, you

will be representing the company when you compete at the battalion

level. So try not to worry so much about what other people will think

of you and just focus on yourself and what you got to do to be

successful. I consider myself to be a pretty religious individual and

when opportunities like this come around, I see them as a blessing from God. So make sure you stay on top of your prayers and ask God to help you be successful. You just don't want to pray when things are going bad for you, you should want to pray and thank God when things are going good for you as well. Once you win the company board, you will probably receive a COA or an AAM, depending on how generous your 1SG is feeling that day. In addition to this, you may also receive a 4 day pass and a company coin. After you win the battalion soldier of the quarter board, you will receive either another AAM or an ARCOM, plus a 4 day pass and a company coin from each company within the battalion. At this point you will begin to see who your friends are and who the haters are.

I remember when I won the battalion soldier of the quarter board, one of my battle buddies commented in formation saying to me "oh, so you think your all that now huh". The way I see it is people are going to hate you whether you're doing good or doing bad and although I do not want anyone to hate me nor do I wish hate upon anyone else, people are going to be people and it's important to remember that. Don't waste your time trying to please everyone. People hated and killed Jesus Christ and the Prophet Mohammed, so how do you think they feel about you and me. After you compete and win the Brigade soldier of the quarter board, not only will you receive all the rewards mentioned above but will also receive a plaque and a coupon book for the PX. You will also have your photo displayed in the PX and Shoppettes around post and be recognized as the winner on the electronic billboards located near the main entrance to post.

The next board you go to is the Brigade soldier of the year board and the post soldier of the quarter board. At this point, you will probably have all of the note cards memorized and now just focusing on current events. The technique to memorizing all of the 300 or so note cards that you will have to make, is by studying them over and over again until you get sick of studying them, then study them some more. You have to think "what is my competition doing right now". You know that they are not off partying and getting drunk every night because they have made it this far. So you got to push yourself. You know, one reason why a lot of people are not successful in the Army or in life for that matter, is because the road to success is boring. If it was fun then everybody would be doing it. That could be why most soldiers don't raise their hand to volunteer to go to the board, because they don't want to do all of that studying. Often times, soldiers will discourage themselves into believing that they are not smart enough to win the soldier of the month board before they even try. Remember the old saying that a mind is a terrible thing to waste and also take into consideration the fact that studies show humans only use around 10% of their brain power, so how much brain power do you think an individual is using if they continuously undervalue their own mental capabilities.

Now once you make it to the post soldier of the quarter board and have already memorized all of the note cards that you have made, take some time to begin learning new information within the Army study guide. I'll tell you, the reason why I lost the post soldier of the quarter board was because I knew everything about the M16 and M4 rifle but I failed to study the other weapons such as the M249 and 240 Bravo machine gun because I thought I was only going to be asked questions about my primary weapon; like I was asked at all the other boards but they switched it up on me. Well after they announced the winners, they had a banquet a few days later to recognize them. I wasn't going to go at first but I changed my mind because I wanted to show respect for the winners. After showing up and being seated at my table, the waiters came around and took everyone's lunch order. I remember I ordered the chicken that day because as I was sitting watching the winners receive all types of awards and gifts from

multiple sponsors and a $250 check, I remember sitting there eating

my chicken thinking to myself "aint this some shit". A few months

passed by and I heard the winners for the post soldier and NCO of

the year both received a Ford Mustang as a prize for winning the

board.

So as you see, there are a lot of perks that you can receive from

winning the boards and remember, all of the awards that you   win will

count towards points[25] for promotion to sergeant and staff sergeant.

Unless you have a lot of deployments under your belt or receive a

bunch of good conduct medals from your years in service, it's going to

be hard to max out your award column. So start getting on the grind

now and get all the points you can while your still a private so that

way, once you hit specialist your just waiting to meet your time in

service and time in grade requirement to get promoted and not

stressing over chasing points

---

[25] The Army promotion standards for Sergeant and Staff Sergeant are broken down into 4 categories which are military training points, military awards and decorations, military education points and civilian education points. Points for deployments, qualifying at the range and the score you receive from taking your APFT will fall under military training

Chapter Ten

Profile Ranger

A sick call ranger and a profile ranger are two different things although they can be classified under the same category and held by the same individual. A profile ranger is someone who rides a profile for a long time. Normally, in order to be classified as a profile ranger one would have to be on a temporary profile and they would keep getting it extended. If the soldier is not careful, they could cause a lot of suspicion and raise a lot of eye brows because they keep getting temporary profiles and don't have a permanent profile for their injury. In addition to this, the commander could do a fit for duty evaluation and have you removed not only from her unit but from the Army as well. It's possible that that's what some soldiers had in mind because their sick of the Army and are ready to get out but if this is not your intentions then you may want to limit the amount of times that you get a temporary profile. For many years I refrained from getting a permanent profile because I didn't want to mess up my chances of getting promoted to sergeant first class because depending on what

type of profile you have, could prevent you from attending certain

NCOES[26] schools which are necessary for you to make the next rank.

In addition to limiting the amount of temporary profiles you have, you

may also want to try and switch it up a little bit by only getting on a

profile when a separate injury happens to you in a different location of

your body than the previous profile you received; or when you

absolutely have to. Getting on profile is sort of like applying for credit;

you don't want to apply for credit unless you know that you're going

to get approved, otherwise it's just going to lower your credit score

because the company running your credit will send it to a dozen banks

to try and get your approval. So by using credit as an analogy for

receiving profiles, the more times that you go to the hospital and

receive a profile, the less your credibility will be worth with the people

who you work with. Although receiving a profile will get you out of

work and a lot of shitty details that no one else wants to do, it may

cause you to be labeled as a dirt bag by your peers and/or NCO's.

---

[26] NCOES: Non-Commissioned Officer Education System. As soldiers advance in their career, they are required to attend several schools such as Basic Leaders Course (BLC), Advanced Leaders Course (ALC), Seniors Leaders Course (SLC), Master Leaders Course (MLC) and Sergeants Major Course (SMC). Soldiers must meet specific requirements before attending any of the NCOES schools.

I know it might be sad but it's true, but like I said before, if you're hurt, then you're hurt, but if your faking it, then at least be smart about it. Now there are all different types of profiles that you can get and some of them may even seem ridiculous but they exist and are being used by soldiers all the time. For example, some of the profiles that you can get are: 1) a no standing profile, which prevents you from standing up for longer than a certain amount of minutes. 2) A no shaving profile. 3) A no gear profile, so you don't have to wear your IOTV[27]. 4) No ruck march or running profile. 5) No walking profile or walk at your own pace and distance. 6) A profile preventing you from living in an austere environment. 7) A run at your own pace and distance profile. 8) A profile preventing you from letting your skin come into contact with the grass. 9) A profile allowing you to sleep in during PT hours and not have to come into work until 0930. 10) The dead man profile which pretty much prevents you from doing anything.

There are a number of reasons why a soldier may want to use a no standing profile, such as if they don't like standing in formation.

---

[27] IOTV: Improved Outer Tactical Vest, is a bullet proof vest which is an enhancement to the Interceptor Body Armor (IBA).

Normally soldiers with a no standing profile will still be required to come to formation but they will sit down behind the formation until it is over. It is important that you ensure your squad leader knows that you are there before you sit down behind the formation because they will report you FTR. Many soldiers will get a no shaving profile because their skin breaks out with bumps after they shave. Some soldiers with a no shaving profile will get caught up by their platoon sergeant or 1SG because their mustache is out of regulation, but nothing really happens to them except that they get told to fix it. For those of you who don't have a legitimate medical condition which requires you to have a profile, don't be alarmed. You can still get one by lying to the PA and telling him that you break out when you shave. The benefit to having a no shaving profile is that you don't have to worry about people getting all up in your face if you forget to shave one morning or if you miss a spot while shaving, you will be silently telling people to fuck off.

Some of the common reasons why soldiers have a no gear profile which prevents them from wearing the IBA is because of a back injury. By having this type of profile, it will prevent you from being able to go to the range. For this reason, one thing that you want to be sure of if you have this type of temporary profile is that you have already qualified at the range, so that way you can be able to ride the profile for some time without worrying about not being current on your ERB[28]. One thing to keep in mind is that your range qualification is good on paper for 2 years and your APFT score is good for 1 year on paper. So in theory, you could qualify at the range and be on and off of a no gear profile for two years before you have to go back to the range again. With a no ruck-march profile, you will not have to go on the ruck marches with the rest of the unit. I remember when I was stationed in Korea, my unit would go on a 5 mile ruck march every Thursday for Sergeants Time training and I've heard of some infantry units having to go on occasional 14-15 mile ruck marches. So depending on your MOS and the unit you're assigned to, can dictate how far and often you go on ruck marches. I think ruck marches are cool and something everyone should experience at least once in their lifetime, but after you have rucked marched and ran for hundreds or possibly even thousands of miles, just know that you can always pull

---

[28] ERB: Enlisted Record Brief, is the form each soldier possess which identifies their administrative data such as name, rank, religion, APFT score, Awards, etc.

out that handy dandy profile to get you out of it when you've had enough and are ready to take a knee.

Having a no walking profile is a cool thing to have because it can not only get you out of doing ruck marches but can also get you out of doing any marches at all. While conducting PT, you will fall out of formation and go with the other soldiers who are on profile to conduct profile PT. One thing to keep in mind is that everyone will not have the same profile as you, and although the profile PT instructor may try his best to help everyone get a good workout, they normally would just have you do what you can to the limits of your profile by doing alternate exercises. For example, instead of doing sit-ups you will substitute it for crunches or instead of doing push-ups you will do military press or the overhead arm clap. Another cool thing about having a no walking profile or walk at your own pace and distance profile is that when your platoon or company goes on a ruck march from one location to another, they will allow you to drive there. I think this is cool because I can smoke a few cigarettes while driving and listening to music, plus I get to save my energy.

I want you to keep in mind that people will probably be looking at you crazy when they show up sweaty and tired and see you chilling in your car, smoking a cigarette and bumping your music, but as long as you don't trip off them, you'll be good. If you are concerned about what other people may think of you, then one thing you can do is see if the platoon sergeant or first sergeant would like for you to transport some of the equipment that they will be using when they get there and/or you could see if other people on profile would like to carpool with you. If you look at the profile document that your PA gives you, if the letter **J** is checked yes, stating that you cannot live in an austere environment without worsening the medical condition, then you can use this to get out of the field. If you look up the word austere, you will find that one of its definitions is (something that lacks softness, is simple and has limited resources). So sleeping on a cot is a No Go. One thing I recognized while being in the military is that soldiers normally tend to believe whatever someone tell them, especially if it's an NCO that's doing the telling because for 1) they believe the NCO knows what he's talking about and 2) they didn't take the time out to do the research themselves. So let's say for example that your injury is that you have a broken arm and on your profile the block is checked that says you can't live in an austere environment.

Without knowing what the actually means, there's a high probability that you could be breaking your profile and not even know it.

If your squad leader said that you have to go to the field even though you're on a profile, then 9 times out of ten you will probably wind up going because you don't have any proof saying that you shouldn't. If you really don't want to go to the field, then one thing you can do as a last resort is go talk to the chaplain but doing so may cause more problems for you than it does benefit because remember, there's no secrets in the Army. One thing to also take into consideration about trying to get out of the field due to your profile is that the commander has the ability to make you go and take full responsibility for you if you get hurt or your condition worsens while you're in the field. My advice is whatever you decide to do, make sure you know what you're doing and you don't get yourself caught up in no mess. Because after arguing with your squad leader and/or platoon sergeant about why you don't want to go to the field and the commander makes you go anyway; it may cause tensions amongst everyone involved for the whole time yall are out there.

A soft shoe profile simply allows you to wear civilian shoes while in ACU's. This does not mean that you can try to find some matching Jordan's to wear. Normally, soldiers will wear their PT shoes when they have this type of profile. Soldiers with a soft shoe profile may not be required to do ruck marches or go on runs during PT, but this will depend on what their injury is for. Soldiers who have a profile which prevents them from coming into contact with the grass will not do PT with the rest of their unit when they are conducting any type of exercises which are done on the grass. What may happen is, if there is pavement around, the PT instructor may have you do the exercises on the ground but if yall are going to be exercising on the pull up bars or climbing the rope that day, then more than likely you will be required to work out with the group. Unless of course, the PT instructor for that day failed to look at your profile and just had you fall out of his formation and fall into formation with the rest of the people on profile. One important thing to remember about having this type of profile or any profile for that matter is that don't go back and forth with your profile. What I mean by this is that if your profile says that for the next 2 weeks you cannot be in the grass, then follow it. If you pick and choose what days you want to do PT in the grass, somebody may notice it and call you out, so just remember that the next time you are on a profile.

Another example is having a no running profile that prevents

you from running during PT and getting caught playing basketball in

the gym or doing the stanky leg in the club. Always try to do the right

thing because you never know who's looking at you. I really like the

late work-call profile that lets you sleep in during PT hours because I

am not a morning person. I guess it's because it's quiet at night and I

can get things done. But if you're lucky enough to get this type of

profile and I say lucky because I was never granted the opportunity to

possess one of these bad boys, then you can sleep in for an additional

3 hours compared to other soldiers who may wake up at 0530 to make

it on time for the 0630 PT formation. In order for you to get this type

of profile, you will have to be diagnosed with some type of sleeping

disorder on or off post and simply asking if they can put it on there

for you. This profile like many others, is meant to help you with your

condition, so don't feel bad if you're diagnosed with a sleep disorder

and given the opportunity of reporting to work late. See it as a blessing

and a tool to help prevent you from receiving future counseling

statements due to multiple FTR's.

The first step will be to see your physician assistant and let him

or her know what is going on. Your PA may do 1 of 2 things which is to provide you with a prescription to help you sleep better at night or refer you to sleep therapy program. Be careful with getting this type of profile though unless you plan on getting out of the Army because if you decide to go forward with getting the profile, then your unit may see you more as a liability than an asset. I mean think about it, would you want to be the TC[29] with someone who may at any given time fall asleep behind the wheel or consciously or subconsciously take a nap in the middle of a gun fight. That's what your leadership is going to be thinking when you present them with this type of profile. So don't do it unless you absolutely have to.

With this type of profile, you pretty much can't do anything. No running, jumping, lifting, standing or wearing gear. If you have this type of profile, then more than likely you're in the process of getting med boarded out of the Army. Depending on the seriousness of your injury and the percentage you receive from being medically discharged, one way to look at it is you can either do 20 years in the Army and retire with 50% of your basic pay or you can do a 4 years and get 50%

---

[29] TC: Truck Commander. The TC is required to be in the military vehicle when it is in operation unless the driver is driving in the motor pool and has a ground guide. Some of the responsibilities of the TC include: ensuring that the driver does not fall asleep, looking out for obstacles in the road and talking on the radio.

for being medically retired for having an injury. One thing to keep in mind is that if you do your full 20 years and retire, you can get that retirement check plus a disability check if your disabled at the time of your retirement compared to only getting your disability check for being med boarded. In addition to this, you can receive around $1,200 and up per month from social security, depending on whether or not you have children.

One important thing you need to take into consideration is that if you get social security, you will not be allowed to make over $15,000 per year. Be sure and check with your city social security office if you intend on drawing social security for details. One last thing I want to mention in regards to social security is the fact that you can receive your social security benefit while you are still on active duty, IF YOU ARE A WOUNDED WARRIOR IN THE MED-BOARD PROCESS. Many soldier do not know this and a missing out on a lot of money. Be sure and contact a lawyer if you're interested in receiving some extra cash before you are medically discharged.

Sometimes it may turn out that your squad leader or platoon sergeant wants to act stupid with you because of the profile that you have. An example of this is having a profile that says you cannot wear your gear for longer than 1 hour. When you go to formation without your gear on, you may immediately get questioned by your squad leader asking where your gear is at. After you tell them what your profile says, be prepared for them to ask to see your profile. After they read it, they may say something like "well it says that you can wear your gear not to exceed 1 hour" and even though you try to explain to them that your body hurts when you wear the gear, they still won't budge. The problem is that the profile that the PA gives you is a generic profile that pretty much says the same thing on every profile that they print off for specific injuries. The way to fix this is by going to see your PA again and asking him/her to change your profile so that it says you cannot wear your gear for longer than 10 minutes. This way, they should not require you to have your gear on or to carry it with you.

If you have an MOS that requires you to drive and let's say that you do not want to go to the field, you can get a profile that says you cannot wear a Kevlar[30] because the weight of it puts a lot of pressure on your spinal cord and causes pain. Due to the fact that you

---

[30] The Advanced Combat Helmet or (Kevlar) is the headgear that soldiers have to wear during training and combat related situations. The approximate weight of the (ACH) is between 3 to 3.6 pounds, depending on the size.

must have on a Kevlar to operate a military vehicle, by having a profile

that says this, will not only get you out of having to drive but could

also get you out of going to the field because you cannot even ride in

the vehicle as a passenger without a Kevlar. I must caution you about

getting this type of profile though because you will be eliminated from

participating in all training, field exercises and possibly even

deployments. The reason being is because if you can't deploy then the

Army does not need you. The way to get around this is to only use this

profile once a year because normally you will change squad leaders or

maybe have a whole new chain of command within a year's timeframe

and they may not be able to see a pattern when they scrub profiles.

Chapter Eleven

Use Your Time Wisely

So let's say your squad leader or platoon sergeant releases everyone in the platoon early or gives you a late work call one day, what do you do? Do you go back to your room and go to sleep or play video games? I will not lie to you, I used to do this a lot myself until I realized that I could be using this down time to do something productive that's going to benefit me in the long run. There's a number of things that you can do in your down time such as doing correspondence courses until your maxed out, enrolling in a college course for your degree or maybe you have plans on building a business. The list can go on and on but the main thing is that you don't waste your time. Remember, Facebook was created in a dorm room when they wasn't in class. My seventh grade teacher told me something I will never forget, she said that instead of looking at the people on TV and playing video games, why not focus on yourself being on TV or making your own video games. She went on to express that the people on television are already millionaires and that

we have to do something to get our millions.

Now, I have to tell you and anyone who knows me will tell you

the same, that higher education is one of my biggest joys in life. I'll tell

you a true story, when I was a PFC, my squad leader was a SPC

because we didn't have a water treatment sergeant at the time. I

remember asking him how could I go to college and he told me I

couldn't. He didn't give me any explanation, he just said I couldn't go

and because I didn't know any better, I believed him. Well time went

by and he became a corporal and I got promoted to specialist. Even

though we had the same pay grade as an E-4, he outranked me. Well, I

later got promoted to sergeant and he was reduced back down to a

specialist and I became his squad leader. One thing I'll never forget is

him asking me for help on how he could go to college. Now I could

have done him like he did me in the past but I guess my conscious got

the better part of me and I ended up helping him out. So I guess the

moral of the story is to be careful how you treat people because you

never know when you may need them one day.

One thing that's cool about being in the Army is that you can

get paid for going to college. When I was going to college to get my bachelor's degree, I was making about $1,350 every 2 ½ months for going to school. If you want to take advantage of this opportunity then here's what you have to do. First you need to go to the education center and pick you up a packet titled, "statement of understanding". Fill it out and turn it in to your squad leader. Now it's going to be important that you stay on top of your paper work that you turn in to your squad leader because he could lose it or forget to turn it in to the platoon sergeant or the platoon sergeant can be so busy that it remains on his desk for weeks before he gets around to having the commander sign it and get returned back to you. If you happen to find yourself in this situation, you can always use the open door policy, just make sure that you inform your squad leader that you are going to see the commander. Although you do not need to tell your squad leader the reason why you want to see the commander on the open door policy, you should give them a heads up so that they are tracking.

Now during the time that your statement of understanding is in the process of getting signed, you will have to make you an account on GO ARMY ED and also make an appointment with an education counselor to go over your goals for pursuing a college education and which major you would like to study. Before obtaining my master's degree in psychology, I changed my major about 4 times from PreMed/pharmacy, to Kinesiology/sports medicine, to interdisciplinary studies to chaplaincy; so don't worry if you don't know immediately what you want to major in. The main thing is that you get started. Now I will tell you that knowing what you would like to specialize in while pursuing your associate degree will save you a lot of time, but if you're unsure, I recommend majoring in general studies because as long as you meet the prerequisites and GPA standards for a bachelors degree program, you will be able to get into the college. Although not every college is the same, this is generally the rule.

So after getting all of your paper work turned in to the Ed Center and setting up your account, the next thing that you will have to do is sign up for your classes. When signing up for your classes, you must enroll in them using the GO ARMY ED portal. If you enroll in your classes on the college web site, the Army will not have any way of tracking that you're in college and you will not have the class paid for with tuition assistance. Now one thing to keep in mind before signing up for classes though is that junior colleges are less expensive than 4 year universities which means that if you go to a JC, you will receive less money than if you were to attend the university. Once you have selected the college you wish to attend and have enrolled in your first 2 classes, the next thing you're going to need to do is ensure that you sign up for FAFSA. The web site for FAFSA is https://fafsa.ed.gov. Make sure that you have a copy of your taxes from last year when you get ready to fill this out.

It should not take you more than an hour to completely fill out the FAFSA and get it submitted. Once your FAFSA is submitted, they will send a verification letter to your school to make sure that you're a student there and once they receive a response stating that you are in fact a student, then the funds will be released to the college. Keep in mind that the FAFSA will pay for your education based on how much money you make a year, so as long as you're not making somewhere around $70,000 per year then you will qualify. So what happens next is that FAFSA will send money to the school for your classes and tuition assistance from the Army will send money to the school for those same classes and after the college deducts the cost of your tuition and fees, they will send you a refund in the form of a check, college debit Master Card or direct deposit in your checking account. The way I look at it, you can get paid like you're at a part time job without having to put in the amount of hours it would take for you to make the

$1,350 every 2 months.

As of January 1st 2014, the Army changed its rules in reference

to tuition assistance. One of the main changes is that soldiers are now

required to have 1 year time in service after their graduation date from

A.I.T before they will be eligible to receive TA. Although this is true, I

believe that you should still pursue your education and use the FAFSA

to pay for your classes. If you're a brand new private and want to go to

college then I recommend you go to a JC instead of a four year

university for that 1st year because it's cheaper and they will allow you

to receive some money back for your refund check. One thing to

make sure of when selecting a college to go to regardless of whether or

not it's an undergraduate or graduate school, is to make sure that it is

fully accredited. That way when you get ready to transfer schools all of

your classes will get transferred, saving you a lot of time from having

to repeat any classes. It's important for you to note that if you fail a

class, you will have to pay back the Army but you will not have to

repay FAFSA. What will happen with FAFSA is that if your GPA falls

below a 2.0/ C average, you will be placed on academic probation and

will be given an opportunity to raise your GPA with the next classes you take before being temporarily suspended from the college. Now

one way that you can get around from having to pay back the Army is

if the reason why you failed the class was due to a military reason. So if

you had to go to the field and because of it got behind and failed your

courses, then your commander will have to sign a form verifying that

what you are saying is true in regards to the field exercise that your

unit went on and you will be excused from having to pay the

recoupment from GOARMYED.

One thing I recommend you should take into consideration if and when you decide on going to college is that you look at the benefits of online education. One thing I particularly like about going to school online is that you can do your homework around your busy schedule with the Army and have more flexibility to study, compared to taking the traditional route of being in a classroom. Another thing that I like about online school is that you can do your homework and study while you're in the field. In this case, all you will need to do is bring your laptop with you and you can use your phone as a hotspot. Another thing you can do is log onto your school web site and do your homework on your cellphone. Another thing I want you to consider in regards to going to school in the classroom is the time that you will have available to go. You can either go during lunch or after work. That's another reason why I prefer going to school online is because of my wife and kids. I like spending as much time with them as possible to include going home for lunch but you can make your own decision though, I'm just letting you know what I do. Now if you don't think that you have time to go to college, I want you to do one thing for me and think how many hours of sleep you get every night. Now if you said 7 or 8 hours then you're getting too much sleep. In order for you to be successful, you're going to have to sacrifice something and cutting a few hours of your sleep may be the best avenue for you to take.

Think about it, if you get 4 or 5 hours of sleep every night instead of 7-8, what could you do with an extra 3 or 4 hours a day? If you do the math, that equals to 21-28 hours a week, 84-112 hours a month and 1,008-1,344 hours a year. Now that's a whole lot of time that you can spend doing something positive instead of sleeping it away. True story, one night I was washing dishes and thought that I have a lawn mower inside of the shed that I can use to make money with cutting grass. So I went to Walmart and bought some blank business cards and flyers to advertise my services. I called the name of the company Sergeant Cut's. The next day after work, I went driving around the neighborhood off post passing out my flyer and business card by going door to door. I started off with a push lawn mower until I saved me enough money to buy a self-propel lawn mower which saved me a lot of time and resulted in more money which I made. I would work from the time I got released from the platoon until when the sun went down and would make about $100-$150 per day. Yeah I missed spending time with the family but my wife understood and I love her for that and for always sticking by my side.

Well to fast forward a few months, one of the houses I put a flyer on, was being sold by a real estate broker who also was in the process of selling other homes within the city, so my business really picked up. Well one day my wife suggested that I should talk to him about how to become a real estate agent and I did. The school only took a few months to complete but that's how I became a licensed real estate agent. If you don't already know I'll be the first to tell you that there's a lot of money to be made in real estate and although it's a very competitive market, you can be very successful selling houses because by you being in the military you can keep track of who's about to PCS and are looking to either rent or sell their house and can also help the new soldiers who are just arriving with their family, because you know they are going to need somewhere to stay. If you decide to become a real estate agent while your still in the military, one thing you should keep in mind is that in order for you to not get into any trouble for soliciting to soldiers, you will have to get licensed on post. The way to do this is by getting in contact with the army community service office (ACS) and inquire about doing business on post. In addition to this, you will also have to get in contact with the morale welfare and recreation (MWR) office on post for advertising purposes. This can get a little expensive depending on the type of advertising package you

select but it is totally worth it and not to mention, it is a requirement

Chapter Twelve

Volunteering

Out of the 7 military values: loyalty, duty, respect, selfless service, honor, integrity and personal courage, I think the one that applies most to me is selfless service. The simple definition of selfless service is putting the needs of others above your own. There are many ways in which a soldier can use selfless service but one of the ways to use it so you can get out of work is by volunteering. Although I am a strong advocate for doing positive things within the community, I have recognized that by helping others you can also help yourself at the same time. Before I begin giving you the details on how you can help yourself which could result in you getting time off from work, let me first tell you how volunteering can help your personal development.

One thing you can do is take on a leadership role within the organization that you are doing community service for. There are all sorts of leadership positions available. I remember when I was stationed at fort Campbell, I had gotten tired of doing the same routine everyday of going to work, coming home, eating dinner, going to bed and waking up to do it all over again. Plus, I wasn't really spending a lot of time with my daughter, so I enrolled her into the girl scouts and while I was filling out her application, I heard them asking for volunteers, so I choose to be the troop leader. Due to the fact that I was a male, I had to have a female parent volunteer as the Co leader. After one of the other Girl Scout member parents decided to volunteer as my co leader, I became the 1st male troop leader for the Girl Scouts of Middle Tennessee.

I had a lot of fun as the troop leader and I was a positive role model for the girls. I remember every meeting that we would have, I would give the girls a 10-15 minute PT session and I also taught them drill and ceremony amongst other things. But one of the main benefits that I received was that I was able to spend more quality time with my daughter. One of the cool things about volunteering on post is that you can obtain the outstanding volunteer medal which is worth 10 promotion points. There is no set standard to the amount of hours or length of time that you must volunteer before you can be granted the volunteer medal. The primary requirement is that it is recognized through VEMIS[31]. Check with your installation ACS office for a

complete list of organizations that you can apply for which are looking

for volunteers.

Another way that you can get out of work by volunteering is by
being the first person all the time to raise your hand for a detail or if an
opportunity comes up to attend some sort of military education class
arises. When you get picked to be on a detail, the only time that you
may come into contact with the rest of your company is for PT
formation and depending on what time the detail starts will determine if
you will have to do PT or not. If this is the case then all you would
have to do is make sure that you wake up on time to make it in for
formation. Now let's say one morning you wake up and its 0610 and
everyone has to be formed by 0620. What do you do? Well don't panic,
the first thing that you should do is call the NCOIC that's in charge of
the detail and let him know that you're on your way and that you left
something that you needed which pertains to the detail i.e. eye-pro[32] or
road guard vest[33]. Providing that you have a pretty good relationship
with the NCOIC will dictate whether or not he will cover down for
you. There's no guarantees that this will work but it's worth a shot. The
only reason why you would not call the NCOIC in this type of situation
is because he or she is not a member of your platoon, in that case you
will need to call your squad leader.

Now after you get off the phone with them, brushing your

teeth and shaving should be the last thing on your mind at that

---

[31] VEMIS: Volunteer Management Information System, this system allows volunteers to track how many hours and awards that they have received.
[32] Eye-pro: All soldiers are issued eye-pro which may come in two forms; ballistic glasses or ballistic googles. The purpose of soldiers wearing military issued eye-pro is so that they can be protected from small projectiles and fragments.

[33] Road Guard Vest: normally orange or yellow in color, this is the type of vest that you see construction workers wearing.

moment because your primary focus should be to get there in time so that you do not get called out of ranks. It should take you no longer than 1 minute to put on all of your clothes. If you have not done so already, I recommend that you time yourself when you get a chance to see if you can get dressed in under a minute. When you get outside, depending on how the weather is, you may find that you have frost on your windows. Due to the fact that you don't have time to put the defroster on and wait for the frost to melt, you should run back in your house and get a big cup or pot of hot water that you can pour on your windows. Don't worry, this will not break your window, I have done this many times and my windows are fine. Now after pouring the hot water on your windows and putting the defroster on to prevent any refreezing from occurring, you notice that it's now 0617 and you have 3 minutes to get to formation before everyone forms up and 13 minutes before the flag goes off and the 1SG has his formation. So now you got to hall ass. At this time, be prepared to receive back to back phone calls, the best thing to do is answer and let them know that your almost there, even if you're not; this way your squad leader will inform the platoon sergeant that your in route. Making this first contact with your squad leader may prevent you from receiving a negative counseling statement because although you may fail to report to your appointed place of duty, you did not fail to report to your squad leader at or before the prescribed time. In any case, this is just a little ammo that could help you fight with in case you do receive a negative counseling statement, but by calling your squad leader and letting them know that you're in route, chances are they will just tell you to HURRY UP. My advice is to play it off cool when you finally get there and not make showing up late to formation a habit because you will force your squad leader to write you up, even if they don't want to.

You got to be really careful when you're in this type of situation and are rushing to work because there will be a lot of MP's out, so one thing that you may want to do is learn the back streets that will take you to your company from your house and also know the streets where the stop lights are located. While you're driving, it will not hurt to say a few prayers to God to bless you that you will make it on time and if God is willing, he will answer your prayer. So let's say you make it in time to your company area with 5 minutes to spare before the flag goes off but see that the only parking spot is for handicap. Take the handicap parking and hurry up and get to formation. When you get to the formation, make sure that you make eye contact with your squad leader or the detail NCOIC so they know your there. After formation, you can go move your car out of the handicap spot so that no one see's you parked there and makes a complaint about it.

One of the cool things about being on a detail is that-that is your appointed place of duty, so when you are released for the day from your detail, you don't have to report back to your unit. If the detail NCOIC tells you that everyone gets to go home at 1500 everyday, then you get to take an additional 2 hours off. If your shift is 1 day on and 2 days off, then for the days that you are off, the only thing you may be required to do is come to formation. One thing about details is that your squad leader and platoon sergeant may or may not be in the loop in regards to how your schedule is ran. If they ask you what your schedule is like, the best thing to do will be to tell the truth. Now it is important to keep in mind that the truth may not necessarily be what you guys actually do every day but what was written within the detail instructions.

I know you may be thinking to yourself, what about if I get seen driving by my squad leader, platoon sergeant or someone within my platoon who knows that I'm supposed to be at the detail right now

all you would have to tell them if they ask you why you're not at work

is that you got released early that day. If you feel concerned about their

suspicion, you should contact the NCOIC of the detail and let him

know what happened, but for the most part you should have nothing

to worry about. The cool thing about going to a military education

class such as drivers training, Combat life Saver (CLS)[34] or Hazmat, is

that most classes are 14 days long. Not only are they worth promotion

points but military education courses will work the same way that

volunteering does; by allowing you to go home early once the class is

over with.

A lot of the classes that you go to will end early throughout the days and may start late because the instructor has a prior engagement that just came up. Another cool thing about going to military education classes is that they may allow you to miss up to 2 hours of class within the 14 days without being dropped from the course. Keep in mind that you do not want to get dropped from a course due to you being late because your leadership will find out when they see you come back to the company without your graduation certificate. So make sure that you keep track of how much time you have remaining of the 2 hours that they give you so that you don't get into no trouble and receive a negative counseling statement.

---

[34] CLS: Soldiers are required to take this course to learn how to give aid to themselves and their buddies. Some of the lessons taught includes CPR, how to check for bleeding and dress a wound. The class is a 40 hour, 1 week course.

How I Became A Shammer

Due to the fact that I'm a big procrastinator, I remember showing up for class late everyday by maybe 5-10 minute's and I was still able to pass the class because I stayed within the 2 hour window. Now I must tell you that the purpose of the instructor giving you the 2 hour window is not necessarily meant as a way to buy you time if you are ever running late but rather for times when there's an emergency back a work such as a urinalysis test or within your personal life such as an appointment that you scheduled a while back and forgot to cancel, but as long as you make an effort to be there every day, your instructor will be able to work with you if you happen to go over the 2 hours.

I remember back in the day when I was a private, I used to volunteer for everything, shit, I used to volunteer so much that I would volunteer to take soldiers CQ and staff duty shifts just so that I could have the next day off. I thought this was cool because I knew that I wouldn't have to really do anything while I was on CQ but maybe clean up a little bit and answer phone calls but that was about it. I remember this used to make my wife so mad when I would come home and tell her that I volunteered to work someone's CQ shift because it would take away time from us spending together, but she would still have dinner ready for me when I went home and I love her for that.

Now one thing that is cool about working on CQ and staff duty is that you can work shifts out with the other runner and NCO that's on duty, but this will really depend on who you have working with you as NCO because they might be cool and do this or they might be by the book and not only require you to be there the whole 24 hours but make you stay awake too. One thing to keep in mind though is if the NCO is cool with yall taking shifts while on CQ/Staff Duty, make sure yall got a game plan set in place just in case the NCOIC or OIC come by asking where you're at. One thing I always have used and seems to work every time is to tell them that you went to the shoppette to get some coffee. It is important that you guys work together on this one though because immediately after the NCOIC or OIC leaves, you should call the other person that's not there and let them know what just happened so they can start making their way back to duty just in case they happen to come back sooner rather than later.

Another important thing that you should do is if and when the NCO tells you to go get some sleep and to come back at a certain time, make sure that you set your alarm clock and make it back at the time they told you to come back because for one, it would allow them to catch a quick nap before the shift is over and for two, because depending on what day it is, if it's on a weekday, then you know everybody to include the 1SG, commander, sergeant major and BC will be coming in and ask about your whereabouts. That's why yall got to look out for each other while you're on duty. Maybe you like your job and don't really care too much about volunteering, but if you're a water treatment specialist like me, then you know you really don't do your job. So by volunteering, at least you will be doing something.

One thing to keep in mind in regards to volunteering for stuff is that every time that you volunteer and everybody else doesn't, means that your squad leader and platoon sergeant will take notice of this and 1 of 2 things will happen. After being the only soldier who volunteers for stuff for a long time, your squad leader may directly tell you that you're not going to be chosen anymore and they will make someone else do it or when it comes time for the shitty details to be completed, you may not be asked to do them. I remember back in the day when I was a private and specialist, I always used to wonder why I was getting picked for stuff that I didn't volunteer for. I used to wonder if it's because they didn't like me or something but then I had to look at it from a different perspective. I thought maybe the reason why I continued getting chosen for crap that I don't volunteer for is because they know that I'll get the job done. Regardless of what the reason is for you wanting to volunteer, just know that it's ok if no one else wants to do it, it will make you stand out. One way of looking at volunteering is by keeping in mind that someone has to do it, so why not let it be you

Chapter Thirteen

Ballin On A Budget

Have you ever wondered why you're family think that you're rich now that you're in the Army? Well I think the reason is because of the way that you carry yourself. What I mean by this is that **you would rather show what you got instead of knowing what you got**. Be honest, how many of you would rush to foot locker or wherever you get your shoes from to get the new Jordan's, or always go to GameStop to get a new videogame. To take it up a notch, how many of yall went to go buy a new car when you graduated from

A.I.T[35]. If you answered yes to any of these questions then you should read further to see what I have to say because it can help you whether you're a male or female. Now it's nothing wrong with wanting to shine but you got to be smart about it. You know, it's ok to ball, just ball on a budget.

You ever wonder why there are loan companies like Omni Financial and Pioneer loans located right outside of base?, it's because they know that soldiers are broke. So they charge you 33% interest when you get a loan because they know you need the money and that it must be for something urgent because you didn't want to have your chain of command in your business by getting an AER[36] loan. These loan the fact that it is relatively easy to get approval for these loans, it may not be a good idea to get one because it will put you more in debt. Saying this to say, don't go out and get you a loan from one of these places so that you can go buy yourself a new laptop or take a

---

[35] A.I.T: Advanced Individual Training, after soldiers complete basic training/boot camp, they then go on to A.I.T to learn about their specific job. Depending on what MOS you chose will determine how long you will stay in training.

[36] AER Loan: Army Emergency Relief. Soldiers and their dependents are able to take a non interest loan out to cover things such as car repairs and to buy groceries. Soldiers and dependents have an option to repay the loan on a monthly basis or in a lump sum.

100

vacation because you're going to wind up spending more on those items due to interest, than what they are really worth.

Another thing that gives our family the false impression that we have a lot of money is that we loan it to them whenever they ask for it. I understand that we all come from different backgrounds and may have family back home that's struggling and don't get me wrong, I'm not saying that you shouldn't want to take care of family, all I'm saying is that you should think like what would they do if you wasn't in the Army. Another reason why soldiers are broke is because we don't make a budget for ourselves. I understand that you may prefer to buy groceries to cook instead of going to the DFAC, but if you know that the Army is taking over $350 out of your pay check every month because you're a meal card holder, then I think you should take advantage of this because the Army is going to charge you a meal reduction every month whether you go to the DFAC or not. The same thing goes for eating out. Most of the time when we go out to dinner or buy fast food for lunch, we don't keep a tab of how much money we spend on a daily basis.

I remember one time I had a soldier who needed an AER loan because he was broke and couldn't figure out why. So I asked him to print me off a copy of his bank statement. After reviewing the bank statement, I added up all the charges for the month that he had spent on fast food and to his surprise it was around $200-$300. One thing that a lot of soldiers fail to realize is that that $6.00 meal at burger king or the $3.00 Monster energy drink may seem like it's cheap at the moment, but it really adds up quickly. Thus, what I suggest is that you make a budget for yourself every month and allocate a certain amount of money to be spent on fast food. The problem that a lot of people may run into is not necessarily making a budget but having the discipline to follow it.

Soldiers may think that they don't need the money and so they don't care about how they spend it. In addition to this, soldiers may feel like there's no point of saving because they can use credit for whatever they want if they don't have the cash to pay for it. If this is how you think right now, then focus on saving up your money for retirement. The other way you have to think is what will happen to me if I got fired from the Army today; how long will I be able to survive on the income that I currently have saved up in the bank before I will be forced to go back to work. Is it 6 months, 3 months or 1 month. You really need to look at your finances and start living frugal. The way that you begin to live frugal is by living within your means or better yet, below you means, because if you don't, then you will be living paycheck to paycheck until you ETS[37] through a voluntary or involuntary separation. One thing that you have to think about when trying to save money is to take a moment and ask yourself these questions:

1. Do I absolutely need to have cable television or can I substitute it for Netflix and/or Hulu.

2. Do I absolutely need to spend $80-$100 a month on that cell phone or can I substitute it for a home phone at a fraction of the cost? I know you may say, "well, I need my cellphone just in case my NCO or someone else needs to get in contact with me" and my answer to this is if they didn't need you while you were at work, then it must not be that important. If it is something important, then they can call you at home and leave a message on your answering machine.

---

[37] ETS: Expiration Term of Service. This is when you have fulfilled your contract obligation in the Army. Soldiers who ETS from the Army will generally receive an honorable discharge.

3. Instead of buying coffee every morning from the shoppette or Starbucks, you should buy you a coffee pot and make your own coffee at home. I did the math and if you buy a cup of coffee every day for $1.50, you would have spent $45 per month but if you buy a big can of Folgers that makes 240 cups of coffee for $7-$8, you can end up saving about $360, per 8 months at 1 cup per day.

4. Instead of going out to eat all the time, buy your food from the grocery store and make sure that you stick to your grocery budget.

5. One expense that we may fail to add into our budgets is the cost for gifts. These gifts can be for anything from holiday presents to gifts you buy people for their birthday. One thing about living on post with your family is that you will meet a lot of other families within the neighborhood who all has a minimum of 2 children. Now you can be cheap like I did one time and went to Dollar General to buy a kid a birthday present, but I don't recommend this because I had got him a ninja sword that immediately broke when he was playing with it at his birthday party. So

to save yourself any embarrassment, I think a good rule to follow is to spend no more than $10 per present per child unless they are really good friends of yours or family, then you can spend a little bit more, but I think on average you will be invited to at least 2 birthday parties a month, depending on how many people you know. If you're not careful you can spend hundreds or thousands of dollars a year on gifts and not even know it.

6. Instead of buying a new car, get you a good used car. The way that you should go by this is by taking time to shop around. You can look through Craigslist to find a good used car but I will say to be careful if you do this because if they say they want $3,000 cash for their car, it could be a setup. So in this case, it may be a good idea for you to bring somebody with you or if you have a permit to carry a concealed weapon, then make sure you don't leave it at home. The other thing that you can do is to have car dealerships fight for your business. The way that you do this is by looking at several dealerships and locating the one with the lowest price, then you can call the other

dealerships to see if they are willing to match that price or beat it. Some dealerships may also offer you a referral fee of about $50-$100 to bring qualified people to them. So if you need some extra cash, don't forget to ask them if they offer referral commissions.

7. For my ladies, instead of spending $300-$400 to get your hair done every 3-6 months, you can get you a good wig that would last you a long time or just go natural and for my men, instead of spending $10-$15 every week or 2 to get your haircut, you can buy you some clippers and shave your head bald or learn how to cut your own hair if it's a fade that you're after. Doing so can save both of you a great deal of money, especially if yall are a couple.

8. Walking or riding a bike instead of driving. One of the cool things about staying on post in the barracks or family housing is that you are relatively close to everything, to include your company work area. I recommend that you consider walking, riding a bike or even carpooling, so that you can save some money.

9. Reduce or eliminate your smoking habit if you smoke cigarettes. You know that the most expensive cigarettes being sold is those good olé Newport's. Them shits are expensive as hell. If you like that menthol flavor, you can switch from Newport's to Kool's or Camel Crushes. By doing so, would allow you to save a lot per pack you buy.

10. Try not to throw your money away at strip clubs and casinos. I remember when I was stationed at Fort Sill, they built two casinos that was maybe a 10 minute drive from base. I lost so much money at the casino it wasn't funny and the hardest part was trying to explain to my wife how I just lost hundreds at the casino. So my advice to you is to stay away from them because if you're like me then you will try to win your money back after you just lost it and risk the chance of putting yourself further into the hole.

One thing about me is that I love making money and building new relationships with people. One reason why this is so is because I realized a long time ago that the Army will not make you rich. Instead, the Army will provide just enough money for you to survive. Yes, it's true that you can be able to buy you a nice house and car, take vacation once or twice a year and keep food on the table but that's about it. If you want to be rich then you got to do something outside of the Army and you have to be willing to make sacrifices. One thing that I've always said is that you got to do what you have to do now in order to do what you want to do later.

You know we all need to exercise, the United States is the #1 obese country in the world followed by China and India. The problem is that a lot of people don't want to exercise. One example I have always used to express this point is, although I need to exercise, I don't want to wake up at 0530 in the morning to go do PT. But if you want to be able to spend a lot of time with family and or travel, then you need to focus on what it is you have to do now so you can be able to do what you want to do later. A lot of people will do things in an opposite manner. They will party and play video games all day instead of staying focused on their craft or whatever it is they are trying to do. I think one reason why people don't do what they need to do or be able to live their dreams is because they don't believe in themselves and because they don't believe in the unseen.

For these people, seeing is believing for them. The way they see money is that if I work 40 hours a week at $15 an hour, then that's

$600 per week and $2,400 per month before taxes. If they want more money, then they work more hours. They can't see how making $1,000,000 a year or a month is possible. That's not a reality for them. One thing is that people are afraid of failure. All their lives they have been taught that if they make a 59.99% in school, it means that they are a failure and nobody wants to be a failure. So they go through their lives being afraid of failing, but look at it this way, if you are a real estate agent and you were 59.99% accurate at selling houses, then you would be a very rich person because you're guaranteed to sell one house out of every two people that you meet.

There's a great saying by Tony Gaskins that goes "if you don't build your dream, someone will hire you to help build theirs". You can't be afraid of taking a chance. Employees decide to work for people because they don't want to take the risk of their idea failing. One of my buddies once told me that you can either answer for somebody or answer to somebody. If you're a business owner then you will have to answer for the mistakes that your employees make and as an employee, you will have to answer to your boss and do what they tell you. If you do plan on starting your own business then you should learn from other people who have already started their own businesses so that you can be successful.

Due to the fact that 9 out of 10 businesses fail within the first year and 4 out of the 5 businesses that made it through the first year will have failed within the first 5 years brings me to this next point. One thing that I always say which is that "you should learn from other people's mistakes so that you do not make the same mistakes yourself". One reason why a lot of people are not successful is because they don't know what they're doing. Some people who are in such a rush to get something done will more than likely mess up, because they didn't take the time out to plan how they were going to accomplish a task. By only having a limited amount of knowledge or no knowledge at all, they will end up being lost in the sauce.

My father once told me when I was a child that every time he looks at me, it seems as though I'm always in deep thought about something and it's true. I think about everything and when it comes to business, I try to lay everything out on the table so that I can strategically plan the best course of action that I should make. One good thing that I learned from the military is to work backwards going from the end result that you wish to achieve and backwards planning.

In my opinion, it is better to spend 80% of your time planning and 20% of your time executing instead of the other way around. I know at this moment your probably thinking to yourself saying "I thought all the chapters in this book was supposed to teach me how to get out of work, why is he talking to me about opening up a business and all this other stuff and the answer is, this chapter is teaching you one of the best forms of shamming which is leverage[38]; by opening up your own business to be your own boss.

Now don't get me wrong, although you will be able to set your own hours if you start up your own company, for the first year or so you might be the only person working or you might have 1 or 2 people working with you but that's it. Why you ask, because when you start your own company, you're going to be very meticulous and careful who you hire because you want to make sure that their doing a good job and because until you build up your clientele, you're not going to be bringing in that much money to have a big group of people working for you, unless they are willing to get paid on commission, then you can have as many people as you like. But for the

---

[38] Leverage: One simple definition of leverage is using other people's time and energy for your benefit. If there is a job to be done and you have 20 men to work with, by all of them working together for one hour it's like 20 hours of work has been completed.

most part, you are going to be doing the most work and putting in the most hours until the time comes when you are able to expand and hire managers who can run the company for you without you having to be there all the time.

Now the difference between starting your own company and buying into a franchise is that you will already have a staff and a brand name that will sell itself. True story, one day I went to McDonalds and ordered my food through the drive through. As I pulled around to the window I saw a McDonalds car parked alongside the curb in the parking lot, so I asked the employee if that was the owners car and if he's here working today and he said no, that's the managers car and asked if I would like to speak with the manager and I said no, I had just wanted to see the owner and he told me something I will never forget, he said that the owner doesn't work. I thought to myself, now aint this some shit. So I thanked him, got my food and left. As I drove away, I began to think more about the idea of not having to work or not having to work in the sense that you and I work. Another reason why I wanted to share a little of my knowledge with you about business is because we don't talk about this or get taught it in the Army and I want you guys to know that anything is possible if you put your mind to it. One idea that I try to live by is not focusing so much on thinking outside of the box but to believe that the box is only present because you created it. The faster that you realize this, the faster you will be able to do the things that you are most passionate about. My Uncle always told me "Which of the favors of your lord will you deny".

UNCLE SHAM WANT'S
YOU

Chapter Fourteen

Invest in Your Education

I know a lot of yall have heard of the Montgomery GI Bill Chapter 30 and the Post 911 GI Bill Chapter 33, but may not really know anything about them. That's why I have dedicated this entire chapter to answer some of the most important questions about these two benefits. As you know by now, the Army gives its soldiers the GI Bill as a means to pay for their college tuition. The GI Bill is totally separate from Army Tuition Assistance and they cannot be used at the same time. Generally a soldier would have to wait about 2 years before they can use their GI Bill and have 6 years' time in service before they can transfer it to their spouse or children.

The Montgomery GI Bill will give you $1750.00 per month to go to college once you get out of the Army. If you decide to use your GI Bill while you're still in the army, then you will only receive however much your tuition is. With the Montgomery GI Bill, you will have 36 months of benefits that you could use for college. If you know that you will be getting out the army soon, you can pay $150 per month for 6 months and will receive an additional $100 for the 36 months of your GI Bill. If you elected to pay $100 per month when you first came into the Army, then you will receive an additional 12 months of benefits after the 36 months has been completely exhausted.

With the post 911 GI Bill, you will get paid BAH[39] for whatever city & state that your college is located in. In addition to this, you will also receive a book stipend and college tuition of $18,600 per year. Unlike the Montgomery GI Bill where you will receive the additional 12 months after the 36 months has been exhausted, with the Post 911 GI Bill, you will only receive 36 months using this benefit. If you choose to use the Post 911 GI Bill while you are still on Active Duty, then you will only qualify for your tuition to get paid and the book stipend. The BAH is only paid out when your no longer in the Army.

---

[39] BAH: Basic Allowance for Housing. Every month the Army will pay soldiers who are either married or above the rank of Staff Sergeant a housing stipend based off of the location where they are stationed. BAH is also based on rank, where the higher rank you are, the more money you will receive per month. For more information, please visit http://www.defensetravel.dod.mil/site/bahCalc.cfm

Regardless of the benefit that you choose to use, I strongly recommend that you sign up for FAFSA because you can let the FAFSA pay for your college and pocket the GI Bill. If we do the math then we will find that the Montgomery GI Bill will pay you $1750 per month for about 11 months because you do not get paid during school breaks such as spring break, Christmas and Thanksgiving. So that will equal to roughly $19,250.00 per year for 4 years. That's a grand total of $77,000 that you will get paid for going to college. On the other hand, if you choose the Post 911 GI Bill, then you will get up to $18,600 for tuition, $500-$1000 Book stipend, plus BAH, which could range anywhere from $1,000- $2,800+, depending on the city and state your school is located at. Based on this information, the Post 911 GI Bill is better than the Montgomery GI Bill.

One thing I want you to know is that you can use whichever benefit you choose and you can even use the Post 911 GI Bill for the 36 months and then switch to the Montgomery GI Bill afterwards for the additional 12 months of benefits. In addition to this, I want you to know that if you do not get out of the military with an honorable discharge then you will not receive 100% of the GI Bill. If you receive a less than honorable, other than honorable or dishonorable discharge, then you could lose your GI Bill and not receive anything that I'm talking about. So make sure you stay out of trouble and keep your nose clean until you get out, so that you don't mess up your future. I tell soldiers getting a dishonorable discharge is like getting a felony because it will follow you wherever you go and could mess up your chances of getting a good job.

If you want to obtain your doctorate degree like me, then here's what you need to do. First, you must go to college now while you're still on Active Duty because you can use the Army Tuition Assistance. If you're a private or just joining the Army, then I recommend that you apply for a four year university instead of a JC, so that you can get your Bachelor's degree. This should take about 3 - 4 years to complete. Due to the fact that a lot of soldiers has not been taking advantage of TA and because of budget cuts, the Army now requires that you have 10 years' time in service before you can use TA to pay for your Master's degree. I know it's messed up that you will have to wait 10 years to get a 6 year degree, but that's how it is, so don't let this hold you back.

After you get your bachelors, you can do one of two things. You can sign up for FAFSA to pursue your Master's degree and they will pay you $20,000.00 a year to go to school. The only thing is that it will be in the form of a student loan because you can only receive the $5,600 grant for your Associates and Bachelors, so it's up to you if you want to take out these loans. The other option is to use your GI Bill. If you save your GI Bill for your Masters and PhD, then you could leave the Army as a Doctor with no student loan dept. you can still take out student loans while using your GI Bill and the good thing is, they will be deferred while your either still in school or in the Army. So as long as you're in the Army or in school, you will not have to pay back your student loans. There are two types of loans that you can get, which are subsidized and unsubsidized. The main difference between the two is one will accumulate interest and the other one wont. So if you finance a car and have a high interest rate, you can pay off your car using your student loans or you can use this money to try and flip it by investing in something such as stocks, bonds or a certificate of deposit.

It is possible that you can get out of the Army and make more money by going to school than you currently are making in the Army. The way to do it is sign up for FAFSA. That will give you $5,600 per year. Then sign up for student loans. Student loans will pay you $10,000 a year for your freshman and sophomore year and $12,500 a year for your junior and senior year. The third thing to do is get on unemployment. By being a veteran, you can claim unemployment for 2 years. Check with your state for specifics. The next thing to do is sign up for food stamps. Back in the day we used to call food stamps "that new money", now it's an EBT card. The next thing you do is sign up for the Post 911 GI Bill so that your rent, tuition and books will be paid for. Based on all of this, you can expect to receive about $42,000-$60,000 a year. Depending on the city and state that your school is located in. so you see, it is possible that you can make more money going to college than you currently are in the Army. On top of all of this, if you're in the MEB process, there's a whole lot of money out there that you are entitled to. For example, did you know that you can receive Social Security benefits while you're getting MED boarded? That could be an additional $1,800 per month.

I know your probably thinking like "yeah that's good, but I don't want to be stuck paying back all those student loans", and it's true, in 8 years you can get $134,000 from student loans, but check this out. If you decide to work at a K-12 school, then $20,000 of your student loans will be subtracted from your student loan debt. You can also do a student loan forgiveness. What this is, is you will be required to pay back your student loans on time for 7 years and then the remaining balance will be taken away. Another thing you can do is put in an application to become a specialized officer for the Army, such as a lawyer, pharmacist or psychologist and have all of your student loans repaid. The only requirement for this is that you will have to serve 4 years as a doctor to fulfill your contract. The good news is that while you're working as a doctor for the Army, you could come in making anywhere from $96,000-$128,000 a year on top of having your student loans getting paid off. So it's really a win-win situation, because you can make a bunch of money and get your education all while serving your country

Chapter Fifteen

The E-5 and the NCO

I know you may be asking yourself why did I title this chapter the E-5 and the NCO and aren't they the same rank. The answer to that question is yes, they are the same rank but they do not all perform the same role within the Army. Why is that you might ask, well the E5 is only in the Army because he wants to get paid. He can care less about any missions that his unit may have. He may openly speak negatively about his chain of command and belittle the soldiers he work with. In fact, an E-5 can care less about a soldiers feelings and any personal problems that they are experiencing. An E-5 will not help his soldiers with their career progression and may even be prejudice towards other races. If given a tasking to complete, he will do it half ass or try to pass it on to someone else. On a day to day basis, he will only do enough work to get by without ever going above and beyond. In the Army, an E-5 is what is considered a substandard soldier. One who qualifies at the shooting range with the minimum score of 23 out of 40 and will maintain a score of 60% in each event while taking the

APFT. Generally, an E-5 will stay in the Army as long as possible because he doesn't have anything better going on for him outside of the military.

The only reason why an E-5 went to college was because they needed the points to get promoted at the time, in matter of fact, it's possible that an E-5 paid someone or had their spouse/girlfriend take the courses for them because to them going to college is a waste of time. The NCO on the other hand is someone who cares about his soldiers and will do anything for them. It is not uncommon for a sergeant to take a soldier under his wing and try to groom them for success. Now there are two types of sergeants: the ones that are cool and the ones that are not. The difference between the two is that the cool sergeant will allow you to get away with a lot of stuff such as letting you do a shoppette run during work hours when there's not a lot of work to be completed. In fact, the cool sergeant may buy you whatever it was that you were going to the store to get as long as you can pick them up something while you're up there. Whereas a sergeant that's not cool will make you stay at work and say something like "you should have gotten whatever it was you wanted while on lunch break etc. A cool sergeant will take the time out to explain things to you so that you can understand but can go 0-100 on you if you show them any signs of disrespect.

Many soldiers will tend to stay away from sergeants that are not cool because they may feel like they are out to get them. One thing that I have learned over the years is that some people will like you and some people won't. It doesn't matter how much you try to please them or get on their good side, they still will not like you. The reason why people don't like you could be for a number of reasons but I think one reason is that they see something in you that they want or envy but can't have. It could be because you have a beautiful wife and they don't or it could be because you are smarter than they are; like me and my old squad leader. You can spend time trying to prove yourself to people like I used to, but then I said to myself, i'm too old to be trying to prove myself to anybody and I mean anybody. I'll say after you have finished all the in processing[40], you will notice who's cool and whose not.

---

[40] In processing: ; When a soldier first arrives at a new duty station, they will have to receive briefs about the installation, get introduced to their company first sergeant and commander, receive their meal card and room key if they are unmarried and/or below the rank of SSG

How I Became A Shammer

For the most part, the sergeant will have your back and will even stick up for you when other sergeants say negative stuff about you. One thing to remember is that you are a direct representation of your sergeant; because it is his job to train you. So, if you're looking ate up then it's your sergeants fault, if you can't pass your APFT or qualify at the range, then it's your sergeants fault. Everything that you do regardless of whether you fail or succeed will rely heavily on the sergeant that you have. Because of this, many soldiers will try to do good because they know if they mess up, they will get their squad leader in trouble or yelled at by the platoon sergeant. The old saying "to never bite the hand that feeds you" applies very well to this situation because as long as you do what you're supposed to do then no one will bother you, but if you screw up then you must remember that shit always roll downhill.

It is possible that a sergeant can become an E-5 but it I have not seen an E-5 become a sergeant before. One reason why sergeants become E-5's is because they are about to get out of the Army and so they stop giving a fuck about anything that is military related and just wants to get out. Due to the fact that sergeants have so many expectations and doesn't really get paid enough money to do all the crap that they do, some may feel that being a sergeant is not worth all the sacrifices that they make on a daily basis. This could be why 50% of all marriages within the Army fail within the 1st year because the spouse is never home. It is not uncommon to hear a sergeant tell you that out of the past 5 years they have only been home for 3 of those years because the rest of the time was spent training or going on deployments. But the good news is the deployments are kind of slowing down a little bit.

When it comes to doing monthly counseling statements, the sergeant will put information in it that is specific for that particular soldier, whereas the E-5 may simply take the data from the previous month counseling statement and do a copy + paste and make sure that they change the date that the counseling was done. There's a chance that E-5's will not even do their monthly counseling's, simply because they do not care. Now the NCO is the Backbone of the Army. The Non-Commissioned Officer is a professional at all times, on and off of duty. A Non-Commissioned Officer takes pride in the heritage of the Army and with the rank that they wear on their chest. The Non-Commissioned Officer will not do things that will put the military or their country at risk. The only thing that an NCO is concerned about is accomplishing the mission and making sure that his soldiers are taken care of.

Regardless of the MOS, sergeants may use their rank and position as a way to get what they want. For example, if a female soldier is constantly late for whatever reason, her male squad leader may say, if you have sex with me, I won't write you up or vice versa, a female soldier can go to her male sergeant or platoon sergeant promising sexual favors in exchange for awards and/or promotion recommendations. This tit for tat[41] behavior is completely unacceptable and something that the NCO will not condone himself in. but the E-5 may approach their male soldiers in this same type of scenario by requesting money, a six pack of beer or some other thing of value for them not receiving a negative counseling. In addition to this, not only will the shady sergeant believe that its ok to receive such favors from soldiers but will also try to cover up any instances of injustice that their battle buddies are being accused of.

For this reason, I believe if you see wrong doing happening within your unit, you should be mindful of who you give this sensitive

---

[41] Tit for Tat: "if you do this for me I'll do that for you" or "if you scratch my back I'll scratch yours's is the ideal behind this term. Although this is a widely used term in the Army, by it's definition it can be used in any type of situation.

information to because they could say that you're lying by making the story up. In these types of situations you may want to consult with your company 1SG, IG or equal opportunity, depending on what the circumstance are. Do what's right but make sure that you protect yourself at the same time. The worse thing that you can do is see something that's happening and look the other way because you feel it's none of your business to intervene.

Chapter Sixteen

Know When To Speak

Your Mind

I remember when I was stationed at Fort Campbell, KY we had a Brigade run and not only was it freezing cold outside but the roads had ice on them that morning. We had to be at the company by 0600 for accountability formation. After the platoon sergeants let the 1SG know everyone was there, we then marched over to the Battalion which was about 150 feet away. Once we got to the Battalion, all the companies formed up and marched to the Brigade where all of the other Battalions were at. There must have been around 1500 people out there standing in the grass with me. All the while that we were standing there, some people were talking, some were laughing, I was thinking to myself how much this is some bullshit. After 45 or 50 minutes of standing out there in the grass, the Brigade Commander finally walks outside with the Brigade command sergeant major.

I remember the Brigade Commander getting mad and having everyone do 20 pushups because no one responded to a question he asked, then he asked everyone "if anyone does not want to be out here raise your hand now, and you already know what happened right, no one raised their hand. We started running and people were slipping and falling, some twisted their ankle, but they kept running in the back of the formation. I know I wasn't the only one out there who felt like this was stupid, but I think fear is what keeps us from saying what we really feel. The way that Brigade Commander was, I bet if anyone would have told him that they didn't want to be there, he probably would have had his chain of command begin the separation paper work. My thing is that some of these leaders need to realize that everyone is not built the same. Everyone can't tolerate the cold the same as everyone else.

I think the first time that I got a cold weather injury was when I was a private stationed at Fort Sill, OK. I remember it was around 0645 and the sun still had not come out yet. It must have been after day light saving time. The uniform that we had to wear was our PT shorts, a short sleeve shirt, PT cap and gloves. I know some of yall may be like what's wrong with that, but the thing was, it was 17 degrees outside.

You see, I'm from California, so anything below 50 is cold to me. Put it like this, when you can see your breath in the air that means it's cold. But back to the story, one thing that you will often hear people say is that you will warm up once you start running and that will be there way of trying to psych you out so that you don't bitch about the cold. I believe that running to warm up is true to an extent, if it's in the 30's or 40's, then this might be true but if it's below 20, then they can forget that shit. But again everyone is different.

One of my good buddies is from Wisconsin, we know him as Snowman. Snowman doesn't get cold as quickly as I do, so I can only imagine how it would be if he were to become a 1SG one day and take his company out on a run in below freezing temperatures. If his guys and gals begin to complain, he would probably tell them to take their granny panties off and suck it up. As I mentioned before, there are a lot of stigmas put in place about what people believe a soldier should be. For example, many people believe that soldiers are supposed to be tough and because of this, a lot of soldiers may not tell you that they have a cold weather injury.

I remember when I was stationed at Camp Humphreys in South Korea, it was cold as hell. They had us bring all of our water equipment to the field so we could do some training. The only problem was that it was so cold we couldn't get the water equipment to run. So we were just out there with nothing to do. Well someone had the bright idea that instead of making chow runs every day so that soldiers could eat breakfast and dinner, we would bring our own food. The conditions out there was horrible because our heat kept going out and it was about 7 degrees plus wind chill. I messed around and got stage 1 frostbite out there. I don't know why they wouldn't let us leave when they found out that we couldn't do our mission. I think it may have been because our platoon sergeant wasn't' fighting for us and speaking with the right people because it really did not make any since why we could not come home; or it could have just been one big dog and pony show[42].

Sometimes when I went to the field, I might only have to work about 4 hours out of the day. The other time was spent playing spades and dominoes and smoking cigarettes. But going to the field is not hard at all. In fact, I get some of my best sleep while in the field. Going to the field can be seen as a big waste of time and resources for

---

[42] Dog and Pony Show: every now and again, you will find yourself involved in what is known as a dog and pony show. This is when you have to do things such as work or training; to make it seem like you are doing something important for high ranking officials. Normally done while conducting a field exercise. The dog and pony show may seem pointless to the individual soldier but may serve a purpose in the bigger picture.

a lot of people because they don't know why they are there. Similar to deployments, I think the hardest thing for soldiers to do is to leave their families. The way I feel about time is that it does not matter if your gone away from your family for a month or if your gone for a year because you will miss them the same although you will be able to see them sooner rather than later. The same feeling may happen for those who do not have families. For these individuals, missing the simple things such as their car, bed or a nice juicy steak may affect them the same

Chapter Seventeen

4 Day Pass And Leave

One thing that I really like about the Army is that every month we will get a 4 day weekend. The reason why we get these 4 day weekends is either because of a holiday or a training holiday. Some of the holidays recognized by the Army that you can expect to receive a 4 day vacation for includes: Christmas, Thanksgiving, Martin Luther King Day and Veterans Day to name a few. In addition to this, the Army is so cool that you even get a 3 day weekend for the Super Bowl. Generally, when soldiers are given a 4 day weekend, it may be from Friday through Monday or Saturday through Tuesday.

If the Four day falls on a Friday, then you will be released from work on Thursday and return for PT formation on Tuesday. Normally what I do and what a lot of other soldiers do is if they have plans to travel out of town during the 4 day, they will get a head start by already having their bags packed and a full tank of gas, so that when they are released from formation, they can just take off.

Every time that you intend on leaving the city and going 250 miles away from the base that you are stationed at, you will be required to fill out a millage pass. The millage pass is a safety measure put in place by the Army to ensure that you're travelling plans are not high risk. Within the millage pass are questions such as: will you consume any alcohol 8 hours prior to driving, will you get 8 hours of sleep prior to driving and will you take any prescription medications before driving. Most of the soldiers will answer everything correctly so that they are not told that they cannot meet their travel plans. In addition to this, many believe that the TRIPS form that you have to fill out and submit with the millage pass is just a way for the Army to protect itself in case you do decide to drink and drive or fall asleep behind the wheel.

Being stationed in the United States is so cool because you are close to family and friends and everything else that you are familiar with, compared to being overseas where you're considered the foreigner in their country. One thing that I really enjoy about being in the military in the U.S is the type of respect that you get from the police. There has been numerous occasions where I was pulled over by the police for speeding and let go once I showed them my military

I.D. in addition to this, it's also cool driving with your uniform on when you're traveling from state to state while on leave because a lot of people will treat you like a star and may offer to pay for your stuff; and who doesn't love free stuff. But no seriously, I prefer traveling in my uniform because you never know if one of the exits you take is full of racist people who may be jealous and want to hurt you not only because of the color of your skin but also because of the nice car that you pull up in. walking around with your uniform on in an unfamiliar city or state to you, lets people know that you belong to one of the biggest and baddest gangs in the world, the U.S Army.

It is important to note that if you ever get pulled over by the MP's and you suspect that the reason they are pulling you over is because you don't have on your seat belt, then immediately after you pull over to the side of the road, put your seat belt on over your stomach and place the strap that goes over your chest behind your back. If your assumptions were correct then when they walk up and ask how come your seat belt was not on, tell them that it is but you cannot put the strap over your chest because you have a profile for a bad shoulder and the tightness from the strap causes you pain. This worked for me and it should work for you.

Chapter Eighteen
Effective Communication

When you are preparing to sham so you can get out of work, it is important that you utilize effective communication. One way to do this is by selecting key words or phrases which will increase your chances of getting out of work. By starting off your sentence with words such as: is it ok, can I, or do you mind, will let the other person know that you are sincere about your intentions and the kind words you use may rub off on them, thus causing their response to be polite as well. Another thing to keep in mind is that when you ask your squad leader for permission using one of the key words or phrases, allows them to recognize that you acknowledge that they are in power. The perfect time to use one of the key phrases is when you guys don't have any work going on, that way it will not seem like you are always trying to leave when there's work to get done. One thing to keep in mind is that you don't want to take your leaders kindness for a weakness, because if they sense that you are trying to run over them, then they may stop letting you leave work to go do things.

When talking to your squad leader or platoon sergeant, it is important that you act as normal as possible. If you normally don't look people in the eye when you talk to them, then don't force yourself to do so by straining your eyes while looking at them. One thing that you don't want to do while talking to them is to look away as if you're trying to hide something by not telling the truth. Another thing that you should practice is not talking with your hands; not only is it common curtesy to stand at ease or parade rest when speaking with an NCO but your body language may hint to them that you don't care. I was told a long time ago that there are two types of motivation: actual motivation (AM) and false motivation (FM). So if you really don't care, at least pretend that you do for the time being.

One thing that you don't want to do is stutter when talking to your squad leader when trying to explain why you need to do something that requires you to leave work. If you have always stuttered before you joined the military then this does not apply to you, but if you do not have a stuttering problem, then you should take your time when speaking to your squad leader so that you do not mess up your chances of getting out of work. The same applies when you are running late for work and have to call them to let them know why you're late. The moment that you start talking fast and stuttering with your words may give them the impression that you're full of shit. So it would behoove you to already have an idea set in place of what you're going to tell them.

To have effective communication will require some time and practice on your part. When communicating with someone, you should already have in mind what you want the final outcome to be, that way you will be able to steer the conversation in the way that you want it to go. One thing that you want to do at all times is to be professional, even if you're not, because you want people to believe you. One thing that the Army is trying to do in order to be more professional is not using curse words when sergeants are talking to their soldiers. Some leaders feel that a sergeant should be able to express themselves to their soldiers without having to always refer to curse words. In being professional, you should also strive to be cool, calm and collective when dealing with people and ensure that you pronounce your words accurately

LEON WILLIAMS

The Shammer's Creed

I am an American shammer

I am a slacker and a member of a team

I serve the people within my family and live the shammer values

I will always place what I want to do first

I will never accept hard labor

I will never quit

I will never leave a shamming opportunity

I am partially disciplined, physically and mentally burned the hell out,
trained and proficient in my shamming task and drills

I will always maintain some beer, some money in my pocket and
myself

I am an expert and I am a professional

I stand ready to sham and not report back to work until the end of the
duty day

I am a guardian of shamming and the shammers way of life

I am an American shammer

<u>Acknowledgements</u>

I first would like to thank God for giving me the strength and wisdom needed to write this book. I know that I have not been keeping up with my prayers but I hope that you forgive me and continue to bless me.

Mom and Dad I love you for everything that you have done and continue to do for me. Mom, I want to thank you for calling the recruiter that day and encouraging me to join the Army. I'm happy that I was able to continue the family tradition and make you proud of me.

I would like to thank my wife for giving me encouragement and helping me stay focused. Baby you have been there for me when no one else was. You have endured the struggle and sacrifice and I love you for that. I also want to thank my children. Everything I do is for you guys and I want you to know that one reason why I wrote this book was to show you that you can do whatever you want in life. Do not let anything or anybody hold you back from obtaining your dreams.

I want to thank all of my squad leaders that I have had over the years, I truly could not have done this without you guys. I want to thank yall for instilling discipline in me and not taking away my rank whenever I screwed up. I also want to thank all of the soldiers who I have had within my squad. I hope that you guys take the good that you see in me and apply it to your lives. You know that I would do anything for you guys if you asked.

I also want to thank all of my battle buddies that I have met over the years. For all the good times that we had and the shitty situations we were able to overcome.

Special thanks to Ratonya Kemp for helping me get this book approved. Thankyou for your support. One love

SFC Radford, I know you said not to write this book but it's all good
Hey Candice, thanks for taking some of the photos for me, I appreciate you so much.
SSG Merrill, thanks for looking out for me and putting me on that security detail for 5 months.

SGT Nelson, you were the best squad leader I had. Thank you for looking out for me.
SSG Tippett, Thank you so much for being patient and understanding with me.

SSG Barnes, my bad for throwing up in your new Armada after we left the club.

SSG Craig, thanks for looking out for me in Iraq, I appreciate it.

SGT Tony Coffee, Thanks for being a friend. SGT Leftler, you're the man

SGT Jeremy & Megan Watson, Thanks for being good friends, we love yall

SFC Massey, thanks for being a good platoon sergeant and trying to guide me on the right path.

Private Mullins, I appreciate everything that you have done while working with me and congrats on the wedding

Private Appleton, I appreciate everything that you have done while working with me.

SGT Douglas, Sham Life. SGT Ensley, SSG Chico yall my dudes, keep your heads up.

Uncle Kachebee: thanks for always giving me valuable advice Uncle Ilyas: you my ACE, I love you man, Uncle Mohammed: I love you man, Ben Yusef, Malik, Omar, Laila, Asya, Big Moma, Br. Ayman,

Lamar, Omar Jr. Idreas, Malika, Malik Jr. Ibraheim, Granny G. Yahya, Johnah, I love yall so much.

Uncle Pop, Uncle Kenny, sister TaMya,

Mom Karolyn, thank you so much for always being there for me and Renea. I also want to thank you for taking the time out of your schedule to look after the kids while Renea and I finished school.

SFC Watson: you my brother, congrats on the promotion

SSG Klinglesmith: I appreciate everything, Soup

Jeremiah and Crystal: I love yall so much. Thank you for all of your support throughout the years and being great friends.

Memo and Kalanni: I love yall so much. Thank you for being good friends throughout the years.
SGT Luna: Let's get it

Ashli Taylor: hey sis, you doing big things, keep your head up.

SSG Evans: you my dude, keep your head up and let's get it.

SGT Brown, Thank you for helping me. I look forward to us working together. I appreciate everything you do

Wayne Wonder: thank you for coming out and doing a show for us. That was really special. Peace and Blessings, one love.

Jay and S.H. my Korean brothers. We do Big Business. Much respect.

1SG Taylor: you already know you're a trip, but I guess your just doing your job.

1SG Joseph, thank you for looking out for me when we were deploying to Afghanistan. You and your husband are awesome. Army Strong

Tony Montana- you was a good soldier, keep your head up.

SSG Watkins & Tisha: you guys are family, I love yall, let's get it.

Ms. Ann: Thank you for letting me run the Club
The Legend, SPC Ketih Barrigar, SGT Dukes, SGM Moreland,
Army Strong

I especially want to thank everyone within the 168 BSB, Fort Sill
OK. 626 BSB, Rakassans Fort Campbell KY. 348 BSB, Camp
Humphreys Korea. Warrior Transition Battalion, Fort Campbell KY.

GO TO

<u>WWW.SHAMLIFE.NET</u>

FOR ALL OF YOUR SHAMLIFE GEAR AND ACCESSORIES

In Loving Memory of my Great Grandmother Granny, my cousin Malika Abdullah, My brother in law Rodney Flannigan, SGT Gayle and SPC Nienke AKA Nitro. Rest in Paradise, I love you.

About The Author

Sergeant Leon Williams has served on Active Duty in the U.S Army for over 10 years. He consistently strive to better himself and is passionate about helping others. He is not only a decorated soldier but also highly educated, currently pursuing his PHD in Psychology. Within 6 month's he was able to finish writing three books; two of which are still under review and has a fourth one on the way.

Sham Life

-To Be Continued-

How I Became A Shammer

Made in the USA
Columbia, SC
05 July 2022